D0455560

Second Dad Summer

Second Dad Summer

by Benjamin Klas
Illustrated by Fian Arroyo

ONE ELM
BOOKS

Egremont, Massachusetts

One Elm Books is an imprint of Red Chair Press LLC
www.redchairpress.com
www.oneelmbooks.com

Publisher's Cataloging-In-Publication Data

Names: Klas, Benjamin, author. | Arroyo, Fian, illustrator.

Title: Second dad summer / by Benjamin Klas ; illustrated by Fian Arroyo.

Description: South Egremont, MA : One Elm Books, an imprint of Red Chair Press LLC, [2020] | Interest age level: 009-013. | Summary: "Jeremiah just wants a normal summer with his dad, but it's clear that isn't happening. His dad just moved to an apartment near downtown Minneapolis to live with his new boyfriend, Michael. Michael wears shorts too short, serves weird organic foods, and is constantly nagging Jeremiah to watch out for potholes and to stay hydrated. Worst of all Michael rides the Uni-cycle. Okay, it's a bicycle decorated to look like a unicorn! This is going to be a long summer!"--Provided by publisher.

Identifiers: ISBN 9781947159242 (library hardcover) | ISBN 9781947159259 (paperback) | ISBN 9781947159266 (ebook)

Subjects: LCSH: Gay fathers--Juvenile fiction. | Stepfathers--Juvenile fiction. | Summer--Juvenile fiction. | CYAC: Gay fathers--Fiction. | Stepfathers--Fiction. | Summer--Fiction.

Classification: LCC PZ7.1.K635 Se 2020 (print) | LCC PZ7.1.K635 (ebook) | DDC [Fic]--dc23

LC record available at https://lccn.loc.gov/2019930074

Main body text set in 16/23 Sabon

Printed and bound in Canada.
0819 1P FNS20

For Asher, Kayla, Jayden, Will, Owen,
Lucy, Teddy, Ava, and those yet to come.

CHAPTER

I stood up on my pedals. I just needed to add space between me and Michael so people wouldn't think we were together, even though we were. Dad pedaled peacefully in front of me, keeping me from making much progress in the whole escaping Michael thing.

It wasn't that I had anything in particular against Michael, Dad's new boyfriend. Except that Michael was loud. And too obsessed with his looks. And, oh yeah, rode around on a bicycle decorated to look like a unicorn.

Neon glitter coated the frame of Michael's bike. Rainbow streamers flew out from the handlebars. And right between those handlebars, he'd mounted a plush, sparkling unicorn head. It had the creepy look of smiling in a crazy happy way whenever I looked back at it. Michael even named the bike "The Uni-cycle."

At least Michael was sweating. I hoped that the ride to this Stone Arch Bridge Festival that he and Dad talked about would wear Michael down a little.

"Jeremiah!" Michael called to me. "Can. We. Slow. Down?" He panted between each word. The Uni-cycle was a one speed, one of those old ones with uncomfortable seats and high handlebars. It was definitely made for rolling, not racing.

I pretended not to hear him, but Dad slowed down.

"Almost there, troops," he called.

Michael finally caught up with us as the buildings of downtown Minneapolis thinned and the sparkling river spread out in front of us.

"There she is," Dad said. "The Great Mississippi!"

"Cool," I said. I had seen the Mississippi

plenty of times. Living with Mom in eastern Iowa, it was a pretty normal sight. But somehow it looked different here in the middle of a city, strapped down by all the bridges and traffic.

Michael's breath was evening out. "There's the Stone Arch Bridge." He pointed to a bridge, the only bridge made of stone that happened to arch over the river.

"No kidding," I said. I was trying to give Michael a chance. I really was. But he was making it difficult.

Now that Michael had his breath back, he started one of his informational speeches. "It was completed way back in 1883. They say the cost of it was equivalent to…"

I sighed as Michael talked on. I had already learned all about the history of Dad and Michael's neighborhood, which library was a Carnegie library, and about the "rich heritage of transit." Apparently, Minneapolis had quite a system of streetcars back in the day. Really useful information.

"Where's the festival?" I said when Michael stopped for a breath.

"Mostly over the bridge," Dad said. "Onward."

As we pedaled slowly into the crowd of people going across the bridge, Michael tried to keep up the running commentary, how the bridge had been called "Hill's Folly" and which depot it was supposed to connect to. I decided I might as well tune him out. The bridge was great and all, but it was a bridge.

And as a bridge, it tended to squish everybody into a narrow space. Since we were cyclists on this bridge, we got to ride right through the middle of the crowd in the twin cycling lanes.

This is probably great if you're just riding. But it made a perfect audience on both sides of us to watch the Uni-cycle roll past. I would have stood up on my pedals again, but the bike traffic was too slow.

Michael finally stopped tour-guiding. I looked back to see his attention had moved on to waving happily at the passing crowds who whistled, pointed, laughed and catcalled.

My cheeks felt like they were on fire.

As soon as we finished crossing, I spotted a bike rack in the park. "Let's park here," I said, trying to sound casual, but convincing.

"We could ride up into the festival," Dad said.

I looked at the distant tents and vendors. "It'll be too crowded for bikes," I said hopefully. It worked.

As I pulled a U-lock around my bike, Michael winked at me.

"See?" he said. "I don't have to lock this baby up, because really who would dare to steal such a noble beast?"

Who would want to? Which was a shame, because really the ride back wouldn't be so bad with Michael running behind us instead of riding that awful bike.

Michael took off his helmet and then put it on the smiling unicorn head, clipping it under the sparkly chin. The horn stuck out from one of those ventilation gaps.

I turned away, rolling my eyes. I pulled my water bottle from the clip on my bike. It was covered in condensation, but already the water inside was warm and tasted like plastic.

"Let's go," I said.

But Michael stood on tiptoe in front of Dad. Michael seemed small standing next to Dad, who had spent years operating machinery at construction sites. At first, I thought they were about to kiss or something, but then I realized Michael was fussing with his highlighted hair in the reflection of Dad's sunglasses.

Dad kept turning his head so Michael would have to reposition his face, both of my dad's unshaven cheeks held in Michael's hands. If my own cheeks could have gotten any redder, I'm sure they would've.

When Michael finished arranging his hair, Dad ran his fingers through his own hair until it stood out in wild brown curls. Then he pulled his Timberwolves hat over the mess, leaving it to stick out from under the edges. I ran my fingers through my own hair, which inherited Dad's dirt brown color, but not the curls. It was mostly limp, and hung over my ears and forehead.

Michael leaned in to whisper something to my dad. I looked away. It wasn't that I minded the fact that Dad dated guys. Sometimes he dated men, sometimes women. That was just the way it was. But still, we were in public, and some things are just too embarrassing to watch.

"I'm walking," I said. "I'm going to the festival." Which did the job of breaking them apart to follow me towards the crowds, tents and vendors.

As we walked away from the bikes, I could feel my pulse slow down a little. We flowed with the people down a brick street until the booths and trailers surrounded us. I figured it must be some sort of art festival. Besides the trailers selling funnel cake and roasted corn on the cob, most of the tents were full of paintings and glass sculptures and birch bark bowls and stuff.

It was crowded, like everything in the city. Or maybe it just felt crowded because I was used to living with Mom in the middle of nowhere.

"Ooh, we have to stop there!" Michael pointed at a stand shaped like a giant lemon. "Festival lemonade is a-MAZE-ing. They load it with cherry syrup."

"You drink that?" I asked, not because it sounded bad, but because he usually only drank purified water and weird organic teas.

"It's my one vice," he said. "Come on, Jeremiah, I'll buy you one."

"I'm fine," I said. "I brought a water bottle." I took another sip of the warm, plasticky water.

"For reals," Michael said. "You need one. It's like drinking liquid radiance."

"I'm fine," I said.

We had to wait in line with Michael until he bought a gigantic lemonade. He took a long gulp, then held it out to Dad. Dad curled his lips around the straw. There was something kind of romantic about the way they leaned together to share the drink. It was surprising to see in Dad.

"Yep," Dad said. "I feel radiant now."

Michael held the cup out to me. I looked away and took another warm sip from my water bottle.

We walked onward through the festival. We passed a bluegrass band, tents selling letterpress cards, blown glass ornaments, and handmade jewelry.

I drifted a little behind Dad and Michael. Michael kept sipping from the giant cup of lemonade, pointing to this and that. Dad kept taking little sips, too. And he was smiling in a way I hadn't seen him smile before.

Just as I was starting to feel totally invisible, I saw a trailer selling cheese curds. I pulled Dad away from Michael, dug into my wallet and bought him some.

"Happy Father's Day," I said, handing him the carton of fried cheese.

"Well, thank you, Jer," Dad said. He flicked one into the air and caught it in his mouth.

"Nothing beats that."

I felt a little better. Better yet, Michael wouldn't eat any. He said he didn't consume anything drowned in oil. He could go ahead and live on his oil-free cherry lemonade planet for all I cared.

As we merged back into the crowd, my pocket buzzed. I pulled out my phone. It was Mom.

"Jer Bear," she said. "How are you?"

I had to press the phone against my ear to hear her in the noise. I also hoped this trapped the sound of her voice. Especially the whole Jer Bear thing. Jer Bear sounds cute and cuddly, but I got the nickname because, when I was a toddler, I guess I was pretty grouchy. I might still be a little grouchy, but Michael didn't need to know about my nickname.

"I'm fine," I said, trying to talk loud enough to be heard without actually shouting. Dad and Michael stepped a little ahead of me, probably trying to give me some privacy, as if privacy were a thing that could happen here. "We did a Father's Day ride and we're at a festival. It's really noisy."

I hoped that would be enough to keep the conversation short. But it wasn't. Mom loved to do these "check-ins" when I spent my summers with Dad.

"Sounds fun," she said. "Boy, I miss you already. How are you? Is Al feeding you? And I mean three square meals a day. Meals. Pop Tarts and Hot Pockets don't count."

"I'm fine," I said. "How about you?"

"You'll never guess what I bought," she said. "Tomatoes. I know you're the one with the green thumb, but I thought what the heck? Why not give it another shot?"

This is what she seemed to think every year. "Great," I said. Probably they would be dead by the end of the week. Mom's gardening skills were almost as sad as Dad's cooking. Of course, Michael took care of that now. He was always making stuff like free-range chicken with braised cranberries or marinated tofu salad. But I wasn't about to tell that to Mom.

Dad and Michael were making their way over to a line of port-a-johns. Apparently the liquid radiance had worked its magic on Michael. He disappeared into one.

"It's noisy," I said into my phone. "Let's talk later."

"Love and hugs." She made a kissing sound.

I hung up.

"Your Mom?" Dad asked. He always called her my mom instead of Laura.

"Yep."

"How is she?"

"She's planting tomatoes," I said. We both laughed, then stood together, side by side, just him and me like it used to be.

Then Michael came back out. "Wowser, I feel better," he said.

Dad threw back his head and laughed, then he went in to take a turn.

Now I stood with Michael. He immediately began to talk about all the festivals that would happen that summer. Art festivals, movies in the park, and something called the Aquatennial. "And of course, Twin Cities Pride is next weekend. Really, the other festivals pale in comparison. Do you like pride festivals?"

I just shrugged. I had never actually been to a pride festival. Dad wasn't really a festival sort of guy. As far as I knew, Dad had never been to a pride festival either.

"I don't think Dad really cares about that stuff," I said.

Michael arched one of his eyebrows. It didn't surprise me that he could do this. "Allen says he's excited about going."

Allen. Nobody called Dad Allen. He's Al.

Michael kept talking. "Allen and I thought we could go as a family."

I stared at Michael. "You're not my family."

He looked down at the ground, then back up at me. I could tell he was working hard to keep the smile stretched across his face.

Dad stepped out of the port-a-john. Michael

and I turned towards him with big smiles pulled over our faces.

"Onward!" Dad said, oblivious.

This was going to be a long summer.

CHAPTER

2

"I don't want you to get bored," Michael said, wringing out a scrubby sponge thing. He wore gloves. Of course, he wouldn't want anything to mess up his nails. "You could help me paint. The color of these walls is absolutely garish. Did you know that in this original plaster, they used boar and horse hair?"

"Wow," I said. "That's really useful information."

Dad had already left for work. While Dad operated cranes and digger trucks, Michael and I got to spend the whole day together cooped up in the small apartment.

Every day.

For the rest of the summer.

I gritted my teeth. Grin and bear it, like Mom says.

And really, the apartment wasn't all that small. It was just much smaller than the house Dad used to rent, especially since there were now three of us.

The old house had an unused "study" and also a yard with trees for climbing and even a creek. And there was the garden. I always had flowers and vegetables growing all summer.

Here, we were stacked into a pile of apartments that shared a parking lot, not a yard. At least there was the small city park across the street.

Michael nodded to a pair of gloves lying over a nearby tote of cleaning supplies. But I didn't want to spend my morning listening to Motown and enduring another one of Michael's talks about the ins and outs of plaster.

"We've got to give the walls a good scrubbing before they're ready to paint," he said. "Allen thought it would be good for us to have a project together."

I faced Michael. "His name is Al," I said.

Michael looked at me kind of funny. "I'm aware," he said.

"He doesn't like it when people call him Allen," I said.

Michael nodded slowly. "Thanks for letting me know."

I stared at him, annoyed he just accepted my statement, and didn't argue or give reasons. I sighed and turned away from the cleaning supplies. "I'm going outside. Get a little fresh air."

Michael raised an eyebrow. "Do you feel

comfortable going alone? I could come with you."

Perfect. I was hoping for a chaperone to follow me everywhere. "I'm fine," I said. "I always go out alone."

"I guess you're old enough," Michael said. "But make sure you keep the building in sight. I don't want you getting lost or into trouble. Don't leave this city block."

I didn't answer, but stepped into the dim hall and down the cracked marble steps, three floors down to the front stoop. The air outside was warm. I don't think I can say fresh exactly. City air smells different. All the cars and people and roads. Even by the river yesterday the water smelled different.

I sat on the front steps and looked towards the park. A bright blur sped down the sidewalk across the street, a girl in sparkling magenta riding her bike around the park.

Maybe I should go get my bike. But riding around the tiny park felt dopey. I wished I had brought *The Grapes of Wrath* down with me. The story was long and slow, but I was determined to finish it this summer. Now that I was almost thirteen, I was trying to read adult literature. It didn't seem like it was all it was cracked up to be.

More than reading, what I really wanted to do was work in my old garden, feel the earth between my fingers, smell the heavy fragrance of the tomato leaves. I looked down at the strip of tired landscaping sandwiched between the brick building and the sidewalk. A few ratty, yellowish-flowered shrubs bloomed out of a layer of crushed granite. In places, sheets of heavy black plastic showed through where the stones had shifted over time.

I stood up again, ready to go across the street to the park. It wasn't a big park, but there was grass and a few trees growing up around the empty bottles and McDonald's bags.

The girl on her bike completed another lap of the park. She stopped her bike and looked at me.

She seemed like she was about my age, but it's hard to tell. Her skin was golden brown, and her black hair poofed out from under her helmet. She smiled at me. I hadn't seen anyone my age here in this neighborhood. I was about to go across the street to try to get her attention when I heard the door to the apartment building open behind me, then rattle shut.

I turned around. An old man walked out carrying a watering can. He didn't even look at me. He tottered across the rocks to fill the can at a spigot before walking over to the gold-flowering shrubs and pouring water over them. He leaned back to balance the heavy watering can. The rocks clattered under his feet as he went from one bush to the other.

I looked back across the street to where the girl had stood, but the sidewalk was empty. I sat back down and watched as the old man watered each shrub in turn. When he finished, he sat across from me on the stoop, breathing heavily.

Beads of sweat sat on his forehead even

though it wasn't hot yet. His wispy white hair stuck out in all different directions, but his shirt was neatly pressed. The top several buttons were open, showing gold chains hanging from his thick neck.

He pulled out a package of cigarettes and lit one. His eyes narrowed as he stared at me.

"What?" the old man asked in a dry, dusty voice.

"Nothing," I said.

The man took a long draw on his cigarette. "Those are Potentilla Fruticosa," he said as if we had actually been having a conversation. He nodded at the bushes, their yellow blooms still holding the sparkling drops of water.

"Cool," I said.

He blew out a mouthful of smoke. "If we don't get any rain around here, they're gonna dry up like figs." He looked at me again. "Who are you? You live here?"

"I'm Jeremiah," I said, holding out my hand. He didn't take it, just looked at me. I continued,

"I live in number 30 with my dad. Just for the summer."

"Number 30?" he said. He let out a puff of smoke and coughed. "Your dad isn't that pansy that's been flitting around here is he? What's his name? Michael?"

"No," I said. "That's not my dad." I wasn't exactly sure what he meant by pansy, but apparently, he didn't like Michael all that much either. I decided that I might like this old guy. He seemed to have good judgment.

The man finished his cigarette in silence. He flicked the cigarette butt onto the sidewalk where it joined several others. With a grunt, he stood up and walked up the steps to the front door.

"See you later," I said.

He turned and stared at me again. "Sure," he said before disappearing into the building.

No sooner was he in the building than the girl on the bicycle appeared again. She walked her bike across the street towards the stoop. She smiled at me, her green eyes bright and alive as leaves. The sequins on her shirt made little halos of light all over the steps.

Normally, I would have been annoyed by someone so completely bright, the same way I was annoyed by Michael. But I think I was just relieved to see another person here under the age of 25.

"That man was Mr. Keeler," she said. "He's mean. On Mother's Day, I was out picking a bouquet. I was going to take one of those flowers and he yelled at me."

"They're Potentilla Fruticosa," I said.

"Oh." She said it like it explained everything. We stared at each other for a minute before she said, "You're new here. Let's be friends." She said it like it made perfect sense. Like it was obvious. Although that had been my original plan, just saying it out loud felt weird.

"I live right there." She pointed at the building just across the parking lot. She held out her hand. "I'm Sage."

I shook her hand. "Jeremiah."

She smiled and stood there like she could have done it all day. I shifted. My cheeks got hot. Because I'm the kind of person who finds staring at other people to be weird, I tried to make conversation. "Why do you ride in circles?"

Sage sighed. "Mom thinks I'll get lost or captured or something if I go out on my own."

I laughed a little. "Me too," I said. "My dad is the same way." Although Dad probably didn't care at all. It was just Michael. Dad really didn't worry about stuff like that.

"Do you have a bike?" she asked. "We could go somewhere. Together. And I bet we wouldn't get kidnapped."

I laughed again.

In a few minutes, I found myself upstairs looking for my helmet and having to explain the whole situation to Michael.

"You would rather ride with a strange girl than help me wash walls?" Michael said with a smile.

As I turned to leave the apartment, he called out, "Make sure you two stick together. And don't go too far. And don't forget to bring water."

"We'll be fine," I said.

"It's supposed to be a cooker today," he said. "You need to stay hydrated. And bring one for your friend, too."

I went to the fridge and grabbed two bottled waters.

"And watch out for potholes," Michael called after me as I left the apartment.

I finally managed to get my bike and all the water through the front door. Sage took a bottle of water and drank about half of it right there in front of the building.

"Is it okay with your dad?" she asked.

"He's working," I said.

"You have to hang out all day by yourself?"

I thought about Michael upstairs scrubbing the walls. I hesitated, but decided not to tell her about him.

"I don't mind," I said, trying to keep it from being a lie. I slipped my water bottle into the clip on the frame of my bike. "Where are we going?" I said.

"Exploring." Sage began to pedal. "Follow me."

I followed her down the alley to Stevens Ave, the street that ran in front of our building. We rode south to Franklin Ave, switching to the sidewalks to avoid the heavy traffic.

Being on my bicycle always felt free, but this time especially. There were no parents. No Michael. And most importantly, no Uni-cycle.

This felt a little more like summer.

CHAPTER

(3)

I sat on the couch in the living room while Michael rolled paint onto the walls. All the furniture was piled into the middle of the room so Michael had space. The air was thick with the smell of fresh paint. I flipped to the next page of the book on gardening I had checked out from the library on my adventure yesterday with Sage.

I couldn't help smiling as I remembered how she used the library. She wandered the shelves, plucking books until she had a stack up to her chin. She sat next to me, opening to random pages, studying them, then moving on to the next book. I thought whimsical was probably the right word for her. I heard that word once and it seemed to fit.

"What are you smiling about?" Michael asked, turning from his work. He wiped a dot of paint off his finger onto a rag. Apparently, he couldn't get his perfect painting clothes painty.

I adjusted my face. "Nothing," I said. I watched him roll another line of white paint onto the wall. White seemed like a strange choice for a guy who rode a sparkling bicycle around the city. A faint shadow of the old peach paint showed through.

Whenever Mom and I painted, we added colors to the walls, turning our house into a collection of paint swatches. Yes, I had a lot of experience painting, but I wasn't going to surrender that information to Michael.

"You know, I'd be on my second coat by now if you and Allen had remembered to tape off all the trim last night."

"Sorry," I said. Although I wasn't. When Dad had forgotten, I purposefully chose not to remind him. "We were at that Shakespeare play you wanted us to go to in Loring Park." Michael had created a calendar with all the "activities" that Dad and I were supposed to do on our nights together.

My name wasn't on the calendar tonight. The calendar said "M&A Cocktail Hour" which is apparently a thing they do with their friends every Thursday.

"Why are you painting everything white?" I asked. "Weren't there any colors you liked?"

"White?" he said, sounding scandalized. "White? This is not white. It's Hazelnut Cream." He set the roller in the paint pan, marched to the printer and snatched a piece of paper. "Look," he said, holding the paper up to the shiny paint.

"See the undertones of golden brown?"

"I see undertones of peach."

Michael sighed. "I think it's going to take several coats. I was hoping it would be done before Pride. We'll be busy all weekend. Hopefully I can get two coats on tomorrow."

I turned to a page about turning and aerating soil. I thought again about the garden in front of the building and all the dirt suffocating under the plastic and rocks.

The door opened. "Honey, I'm home." Dad walked in, adding the smell of engine oil and leather into the already full air.

"I can't believe it's that time already," Michael pecked him a kiss. "I'm already late. I've got to throw together something for supper."

"It's looking good in here," Dad said. "I didn't know you picked white."

"Hazelnut Cream," Michael said.

"That's exactly what I meant," Dad said. He went to shower and Michael's arms moved faster, frantically trying to finish off the wall.

There was something kind of sad and desperate about it.

I sighed. "I can do that. You can go make supper."

"You know how?" Michael stopped, staring at me.

"More or less," I said. I definitely knew better than he did, zigzagging paint all over the place. "I've painted six or seven rooms at Mom's house."

Michael arched an eyebrow. He was probably wondering why I had waited so long to admit this, but he sighed, shrugged and handed me the roller.

I heard him clunking around the kitchen while I rolled. I had to admit that I liked rolling paint. I liked the stick of the paint, the way it left the wall looking perfect and clean. I moved the roller up and down the wall in long lines, each one extending the wet edge of the paint. I finished and was wrapping up the supplies as Michael brought a new smell to the table.

Dad walked out, wrapped in a towel. "What's cookin' good lookin?"

Michael waved his arms over the pile of pasta like the woman on *Wheel of Fortune*. "This is the new kale, hemp and flaxseed pesto from Real Foods."

When we sat down to eat, it was annoyingly good.

After supper, Michael washed the dishes and I dried. Dad stood in the doorway to the kitchen. The bulk of him nearly filled the frame.

"I just got a call," he said. "Mary and Jo can't host cocktails tonight; Emma came home from daycare with a temperature."

"Allen," Michael dropped the plate he was washing back into the sink. "Please don't tell me you volunteered us."

"Why not?" Dad shrugged.

"Are you serious?" Michael's voice was higher. "Have you noticed the living room? The walls are wet. Our furniture is pretending to be Mount Everest."

"We can slide it back to make space." Dad shrugged. "It'll be fine."

Michael stood with his hands on his hips. "What am I supposed to serve for drinks?"

Dad opened the fridge. "We've got a few beers. Some of this kombucha stuff. It'll be fine."

"It'll have to be." Michael said it as though there was no way it would be fine.

Dad wrapped his thick arms around Michael. "It'll be fine."

Michael relaxed a little, then strained against Dad's strong arms. "I need to finish washing the dishes."

Dad released him. "I'll set up the living room," Dad said.

As Dad left the kitchen, Michael shot me an exasperated look. I actually felt the same way about Dad's spontaneity. He was always doing things like this, just flying by the seat of his pants. It drove me nuts, but there was no way I was going to show that to Michael.

I shrugged. "It's not a big deal. It's not like he's

springing a dinner party on you or something."

Michael shook his head. "If he ever does that, I swear to…"

Dad returned the living room to a state of usability, keeping everything a safe distance from the walls. I pulled in some extra chairs. Michael produced a platter of chips and salsa and set out a neat row of glasses.

"We probably won't need the beers," Michael said. "The paint fumes are probably enough to get anyone tipsy." Michael froze. "Heather! Heather is pregnant."

He and Dad rushed to collect all of the fans from around the apartment. They made the living room feel like standing inside a tornado. The fumes blew away. Or, at least, most of them.

Pretty soon, the buzzer rang and people started filling the apartment. At his old place, Dad had a few friends from work, but nothing like this group. His old friends were a lot more…boring, for lack of a better word. Normal. His old friends looked more normal.

As the people came in, they all shook my hand and introduced themselves.

Emily had short, spiky hair and arms covered in star tattoos. She came in with someone named Robi, who I wasn't sure was a man or woman. Robi had a wispy beard, but also boobs.

A woman named Sarah pulled me into a hug. Beads hung from her dreadlocks.

Jonathan and Ben looked older, their hair dusted with gray. They were perfect opposites. Jonathan was short with pasty white skin. Ben was tall, his gray hair bright against his dark brown skin.

"Little Jon and Big Ben," Ben said. "Robin Hood and the clock. It's the easiest way to remember us."

"Big Ben is actually the name of the bell, not the clock," Michael said.

Heather waddled in, obviously very pregnant. She pointed at the walls of the living room. "Cute color, Michael," she said. "Like cream and hazelnuts. I want to pour your walls into my coffee." She disappeared into the bathroom. Dave, her husband, followed her, saying that Heather needed his help to get up off the toilet these days.

"See?" Michael said to Dad. "She gets it."

Then Michael leaned close to me. "She helped me pick out the color."

When Heather and Dave came back into the room, Dave shook my hand and introduced himself as "Dave. The straight one." Everyone else laughed.

As they all settled in, Michael got them all something to drink. I stood at the edge. Dad invited me to sit with them, but I left to go outside.

"Don't go too far," Michael said as I left. "It will be dark soon."

I went across the street to the park, lying down on the prickly grass. Looking up at the building, I could see the shapes of people in the apartment. Dad had friends now. Something about the thought made me feel a little jealous.

I pulled a handful of grass and tossed it into the air. I lay back and watched the clouds moving. The sun was behind the line of buildings now, leaving the park cool and shady. I closed my eyes.

"What's up?"

I opened my eyes. Sage stood over me.

"You're bored a lot, aren't you?" I asked her.

She laughed. "Yes." She laid back beside me.

I looked back at the shapes of people in the apartment building. Then I looked over at Sage. Maybe I was getting a friend, too.

I wished I could tell her about Michael and how annoying he was and how right that very minute, my dad was upstairs with a whole group of new friends. For some reason, though, I still didn't want her to know any specifics about Dad or that he had a boyfriend.

I wondered how long I would be able to keep the secret.

She stared up at the sky. "Look at all these clouds," she said. "Sometimes I name them."

I stared at her, not sure what to say.

She went on, her face still turned to the sky. "I like to think what type of personalities they have. Like that one. It's big and squishy. Maybe Erma. She's always baking things for the other clouds. They go to her when they're sad. She probably hugs them while they rain."

I laughed a little.

"Is that weird?" she asked.

"Yeah," I said, but I looked up at the clouds with her. We watched them float across the dusky sky.

"Iggy," she said, pointing to a small one. "He's Erma's grandson. Great grandson maybe. He's her favorite, although she would never admit it to the other clouds."

I tried to see what she was seeing. To me, all the clouds just looked like clouds. Water vapor.

"That one." Sage pointed to another cloud. "That one is a Jeremiah. It has very precise edges."

I smiled, my cheeks burning a little. I could

tell which cloud she was looking at. It was lower than the others, compact, not one of those sprawling wispy clouds.

CHAPTER

"Hey, Jer Bear," Mom's voice called from
the phone. "How's the weather up there? Iowa's
got a heat wave. And the humidity! I feel like
I'm swimming just walking through the yard."

I leaned back against the bricks on the stoop
of the apartment building. Even from down
here I could smell the fumes from the third-floor

apartment where Michael was rolling another coat of paint.

"Are you watering your tomatoes?" I asked.

"Um, I am now." She laughed. "God, we'll have to see whether or not this garden is going to last. Let's face it. I'm not the best at this kind of stuff."

"You're fine."

"What did you eat for supper last night?" she asked.

It was my turn to laugh. "Kale, hemp and flaxseed pesto."

The door behind me opened, and out came Mr. Keeler with the watering can. He didn't even look at me as he walked to the spigot. He chose careful footsteps through the uneven, rocky garden. He sounded like his lungs had to work hard. Probably from all the smoking.

Mom was laughing into the phone.

"I'll talk to you later," I said.

"Love and kisses, Jer Bear!"

I hung up, blushing a little, but Mr. Keeler

didn't seem like he heard anything.

As he poured water over the first shrub, I walked over the rocks to him.

"I can help," I said, holding out my hand.

He narrowed his eyes. "I've been watering these bushes for fourteen years." But he handed me the watering can and walked back to sit on the stoop. His breathing evened out while I finished the job.

"Lousy garden," Mr. Keeler said. "These bushes haven't grown much since they put in the plastic and rocks. Some idiot landscaper." He pulled out a cigarette and lit it. I set the watering can down by his feet.

Just then, Michael stepped out of the building. He wasn't in his paint clothes now. He wore a teal tank top and short-shorts. An empty canvas bag hung from his shoulder like a purse. He looked at me, then Mr. Keeler. He pulled a tight smile across his face.

"Good morning, Mr. Keeler." Michael said, his voice sounding as forced as the smile.

I looked over at Sage's building, hoping she wouldn't see Michael.

"Pansy," Mr. Keeler muttered at Michael. Mr. Keeler ground the end of his cigarette into the concrete stoop, then flicked it onto the sidewalk.

Michael stared at the cigarette butt. "I'm sure you haven't seen this, but they have a receptacle right here for you," said Michael pointing at a coffee can half filled with sand and cigarette butts.

Mr. Keeler leaned back against the rough bricks. "I've seen it," he said.

Michael glared at Mr. Keeler for a long time. Mr. Keeler just stared right back, half a smirk on his face.

Eventually, Michael turned to me. "I was just about to hop out for a few groceries," Michael said. "Care to join?"

"I think I'll sit here for a while," I said. "With Mr. Keeler. He was telling me about the garden."

Michael frowned. "I'm sure that's

enlightening. You have your apartment key?"

"Yes."

Michael looked concerned. "You're sure you'll be okay here by yourself?"

"Yes."

Michael sighed and walked down the sidewalk.

Mr. Keeler turned to me. "That's your dad?" He asked.

"No," I said. I was quiet for a minute, then made myself add, "That's his boyfriend."

Mr. Keeler nodded. "You don't like him, eh?"

I shrugged. "I don't know."

"You know," he said. "If there's one thing I've learned in this lousy world, it's that you've got to stand your ground. If you don't like him, get rid of him. If you're not careful, he might be around for good."

"Yeah," I said.

Mr. Keeler hauled himself to his feet. "Too bad about this garden," he said. "It used to be full of daylilies. Every August it looked like the garden bed was on fire with all the blooms." He fumbled with the door before going inside.

Later that day, Sage and I met up with our bikes in the alley.

"Watch out for potholes," I told her, thinking of Michael's warnings. I meant to say it as a joke, but Sage rolled her eyes.

"That's what Mom always says."

We rode up and down the streets of our neighborhood, passing other brick buildings. We rode past Open Arms, Michael's church that he dragged Dad and me to. We passed Marzetti's Hardware.

As we rode, I tried to piece together a map in my head of all the things I saw. It would be useful to know where things were in the neighborhood. We rode until Sage said her legs were tired. So were mine. We stopped at General Dollar for drinks. I bought a bottle of iced tea. Sage chose fruit punch.

We brought our drinks back to the park. As we sat on the grass, Sage kept naming clouds, but I was distracted. I wondered whether Mr. Keeler was right. Should I do something to get rid of Michael? What would I do?

I was still thinking about this when Dad and I went for another ride that night. My legs ached. I didn't use a bike much during the school year. This week, I had already used it a ton. Still, the ache felt good. My muscles were getting stronger.

I followed Dad down the alley. He didn't feel the need to tell me to watch out for potholes.

The tall buildings cast long shadows over the road. I followed Dad as he led me straight down Stevens Ave. The tires hummed. I was thankful I had been riding around with Sage. Dad's long legs kept a steady pace that was difficult to match.

Eventually, we pedaled down Nicollet until it dead-ended, and Dad led me onto a ramp. We coasted down into a sort of bicycle highway.

"Midtown Greenway," Dad said.

We merged into the bicycle traffic. We rode

west, surrounded by other cyclists, joggers, and skaters.

The Greenway was down in a rut that ran beneath roads up ahead. It probably used to be train tracks or something that they paved over.

We passed several ramps, then pulled over. Dad got off his bike, pointing to the sign. The Girard Street exit.

"This is where I first met Michael face to face." he said. "Last year, during the art festival, remember? We both rode in because he said the parking would be insane. He wanted a quieter place to meet."

Last year. I remembered the day Dad left for the date. He had spent weeks emailing Michael, after they met online. When they finally decided to meet in person, Dad had been all jittery.

I had spent the day with a friend at Lake Nokomis. It wasn't unusual for Dad to have occasional dates back then, but when he came back from this one, I knew something was different. Dad was a little lighter on his feet. His eyebrows and the edges of his mouth were just a little bit raised.

Standing here a year later, his face was all lit up with the memory.

"I remember," I said. Dad was happy. He was really happy with Michael. I couldn't take that away from him. I couldn't try to get rid of Michael. Still, there was no reason I had to like Michael. All I had to do was tolerate him for the rest of the summer. I thought I could probably do that.

Dad swung his leg up over his bike. We merged back onto the Greenway until we came up to Lake of the Isles. We followed a smaller trail around the lake, then went through a tunnel that led out to another lake. The sign said it was called Bde Maka Ska. Dad said it was a Dakota name, and that you said it like, "beh-DAY mah-KAH skah." Wind blew over the water. It glittered so bright I wished I had brought my sunglasses.

We rode until we came to a beach. We locked

our bikes and walked down to the water. Dad pulled off his shoes and socks. So did I. We stood on the edge of the lake. Gentle waves licked our toes.

"Tomorrow's the Pride Festival," Dad said.

"Since when do you go to Pride things?" I said.

Dad smiled. "Since Michael. It's important to him."

I hesitated, looking out over the sparkling water. "Is it important to you, too?"

"Yeah," Dad said. "It's becoming more important anyway."

"Why?" I asked.

Dad picked up a stone and skipped it out over the water. "Lots of reasons. Michael, first of all. But I haven't really had time in my life where I expressed that part of me. My bisexuality. It's always been there, something I wanted to think of as normal. I guess now I'm starting to think important stuff shouldn't just be normal. It should be special."

We walked across the sand, back to our bikes. As we unlocked them Dad said, "What do you think of Michael?" Dad's face was bright, obviously expecting Michael and me to be best friends after a whole week together.

I thought about Michael's perfect hair, the way he blared his Motown music, his stupid Unicycle, his constant factoids and reminders. "He's fine." I said. Then I remembered the name thing. "He calls you Allen."

Dad smiled. "Yeah, I know."

"You don't like it when people call you that."

Dad blushed a little. He scratched behind his ear. "I guess I don't mind. It's different coming from him."

I made myself smile. "Good. I'm glad it doesn't annoy you." But it sure as heck annoyed me.

CHAPTER

5

Michael owned an entire crate of rainbow stuff that he slid out from under the bed. A vest, several hats, caps, visors, lanyards, shirts, even feather boas. Of course, I probably shouldn't have been surprised by this.

Michael smiled at my wide eyes. "Just collected a little here and there over the years.

It's hard not to at these festivals." He picked up a pair of rainbow pompoms, shaking them like he was about to give a cheer. "Sometimes, you've just got to wave that pride. You can pick something out to wear to the festival today."

Although I already knew I was going to say no, I couldn't help digging through the bin. It was like stirring a giant bowl of sprinkles. I found several bracelets, one with horizontal rainbow stripes, one with a rainbow of hearts, one made out of rubber with the word PRIDE stamped into it.

I looked at Michael's wrist resting lightly on the edge of the box. He wore a rainbow bracelet made of sparkling stones.

"You should wear a hat." Michael picked out a bucket hat with a rainbow flag stitched onto it.

"What's all this?" Dad asked, walking into the room. I dropped the bracelet I was holding.

Michael waved his hand over the items. "A box of wonder and magic. Pick something for the festival."

Dad chuckled. "You got any bi-pride in there? You know we have our own flag, right?"

"The rainbow is broad." Michael said. "I was trying to get Jeremiah to wear one of these hats, and I haven't heard that he's gay. Rainbows are all about pride and alliance. Anybody can join."

Dad just walked towards the door. "I'm ready when you are. Onward, troops!"

I stood up.

Michael sighed. "Alright," he said. "I suppose." He rummaged through the box. "Here's something for you, dear."

He threw a feather boa at Dad. Dad took it and tied it around his neck. It drooped from his shoulders.

Michael sighed. "Not an ounce of glamor in you." He pulled the boa off Dad's neck and we walked down the steps.

"We could ride our bikes," Michael said.

I thought of the Uni-cycle down in the basement next to my bike. "Let's walk," I said. "My riding muscles are sore."

The day was warm and humid, probably going to become hot. By the time we were walking down Nicollet Avenue, I realized I should have brought a water bottle.

Michael started another one of his tour guide talks.

"The first Twin Cities 'pride festival' was held way back in 1972," he said. "It was just a group of students hosting a picnic in Loring Park celebrating the 3rd anniversary of the Stonewall Riots. It's grown to way more than 100 students now. It lasts three days, and now there's the Ashley Rukes Pride Parade down Hennepin on Sunday."

As he started talking about the role of corporate sponsorships in the festival, I tuned him out. A few more blocks and we were at Loring Park. It was already full of people wandering around between the booths and tents. Several stages were set up. Bands plunked out loud notes.

As we walked into the festival, I realized we

probably didn't look much like a group. I had my blue t-shirt and cut offs. Dad wore a brown t-shirt and jeans. Dad looked extra big walking next to Michael. Michael wore his rainbow bracelet, *Born This Way* tank top, and short shorts with the types of holes and wrinkles that only happen in expensive factories.

Right away, Michael bought one of those huge festival lemonades, cherry flavored.

"Want one?" he asked.

"I'm fine," I said.

"I'm buying," said Michael.

"I'm not thirsty," I lied.

"I've got the money," Michael insisted. "And it's already so muggy."

"Really," I said. "I'm fine."

After buying his lemonade, Michael held it in one hand, holding Dad's hand in the other.

Dad leaned toward him for a sip. "Radiant," he said. They both laughed.

I trailed behind them a little as we walked between the booths. Unlike the Stone Arch

Festival, these tents weren't filled with art, but with all sorts of community resources and organizations: PFLAG, Out Front Minnesota, Gay Straight Alliance. I had to work to stay close to Dad through all of the people now filling the park.

Michael was the kind of person who was at home here. He pulled Dad along from table to table, tossing his head to the music that now seemed to come from everywhere, crowding the park with noise. Dad stayed next to Michael, sharing the stupid cherry lemonade.

At the Human Rights Campaign table, they were giving out blue bags with large yellow equals signs on them. Michael made me take one.

"You'll need it," he said. "You can pick up some serious giveaways here."

We passed banners from churches, gay rights organizations, and all sorts of others, including the city transit system and several politicians. My bag started to collect candy, fliers, bracelets, and tattoos with store logos stamped into a rainbow pattern. Michael made sure I took each of the promotional granola bars from the Real Foods booth.

We stopped so Dad and Michael could chat with the people at the Open Arms table, Michael's church. Pastor Veronica shook my hand and even remembered my name.

Finally, we approached a large booth that was all pink, purple, and blue.

"Here you go," Michael said. "We should stop here. Get you some swag."

The banner said, "Bisexuals of Minnesota." When Dad had said bisexuals had their own flag, I thought he had been teasing, but they really did. It struck me how little I knew about Dad being bisexual. I always just kind of lumped it in with gay. Or maybe gayish. Mom called it "Diet Gay," but it wasn't.

Dad and Michael walked under the cover of the tent. I was about to follow them when someone called my name.

I recognized that voice. It was Sage. What was she doing here?

Suddenly she was standing right next to me. Her black hair was huge in the humid air and tied behind her head in a bunch about the size of a soccer ball. Seeing that she wasn't wearing any rainbows, I was extra thankful that I wasn't either. Her shirt said HMONG PRIDE in big bold letters above a flower-like symbol. Like Michael, she carried a giant cherry lemonade.

"What are you doing here?" she asked. "Are you here with your dad?"

I was about to point him out to her, but when I looked over, Michael and Dad were standing arm in arm looking over all the bi pride stuff. For some reason I froze up and didn't want Sage to see them.

I stared at her. Would she be weird about it? Maybe I should wait until I knew her a little better before trying out information on her like that.

"I'm here with my Dad." I looked around, like

I didn't know where he had gone. "He's around here somewhere."

"Is he...?" her voice trailed off.

I knew what she was asking. I tried to think of some way to casually change the subject. I looked down at my feet, frustrated at myself for not being open and matter of fact.

"So," I said, still looking for a way to change the subject. I pointed to her shirt. "What's Hmong Pride?"

"It's a group for Hmong people on the LGBTQ spectrum."

"The what?" I hated admitting that I didn't know these things.

"LGBTQ." Sage repeated. "Lesbian. Gay. Bisexual. Trans. Queer." Sage looked at me intensely, like she was trying to read me. "My Hmong mom is a lesbian. My other mom is queer."

Moms. Sage had moms.

I just stood there staring at her. A million things bubbled up inside me. I thought of how I had tried to hide the fact that Dad was bi. How I did my best to ensure she wouldn't know about Michael. How thankful I had been that I wasn't wearing any rainbows.

I opened my mouth but couldn't think of anything to say.

"I've got to get back to the booth," Sage said, turning to go. I watched her until she disappeared into the crowd.

CHAPTER

6

I stood there for another minute. Sage had moms. Like I might have dads one day. Why was I so stupid, trying to hide Dad like he was something to be embarrassed about? Now Sage probably thought I was a person who couldn't handle it.

I joined Dad and Michael in the Bisexuals of

Minnesota booth. The woman at the table was trying to get Dad to add his email address to a list. When she saw me, she gave me a sticker with the bi flag on it. Like I was a little kid who was supposed to like stickers or something. I slid it into my bag.

As we moved on, Michael turned to Dad. "You're sure you don't want to get something?"

Dad shrugged. "Nothing caught my eye."

I wanted to point out that not everyone had to flaunt themselves like Michael did but thought better of it. Again, we joined the river of people flowing through the park.

One of the families we passed had a boy about my age wearing a shirt that said "I Heart My Dads." The boy and I nodded at each other, like we knew each other on some level. Then we walked on, not speaking. Did Sage share that type of knowing, too?

Near the pond, an altar was set up. Michael informed me that it was for "impromptu commitment ceremonies."

When we got close to the altar, Dad got down on one knee. Michael gasped. Dad tied his shoe. Michael kicked him but also laughed.

Clearly, Michael was winning the day.

"I'm getting thirsty," I said, regretting the words almost as soon as I said them. Now Michael was going to get to do the I-told-you-so thing.

"I could use a refill anyways," said Michael. He pulled me to the nearest lemonade stand. Somehow, the way that he didn't rub it in was even more frustrating.

"A refill," Michael said, rattling the ice in his cup, "And a large cherry lemonade for my young compatriot."

"Just plain," I called over his shoulder.

When Michael handed me the large cup, I mumbled a thank you.

After we had our drinks, Dad led the way to an empty table. I was surprised to see Mr. Keeler sitting nearby.

A cigarette hung from his frowning mouth.

His face looked like he would rather be anywhere else besides the festival, but he wore tons of rainbow stuff. Unlike Michael's bin of pride swag, Mr. Keeler's rainbows looked old. Weathered. And some of them had two extra colors, the rainbow with hot-pink and turquoise added to the stripes.

His rainbow t-shirt was faded almost pastel and his rainbow visor had a crease down the middle. The rainbow suspenders hung slack from his shoulders as he leaned forward with his cigarette.

I hadn't expected Mr. Keeler to be gay, especially with how he called Michael a pansy.

Dad nodded to Mr. Keeler. "Happy Pride."

Mr. Keeler just nodded and released a mouthful of smoke.

I could tell Michael was agitated. I was beginning to figure out he always got this way around Mr. Keeler. As we drank our lemonades, Michael kept shooting looks back at Mr. Keeler.

Dad rested his hand on Michael's leg. "Let it

go," he said. "Someone else can deal with it."

Michael pulled a smile across his face. We sat for a few minutes in peace, the buzz of the festival filling the air.

Suddenly Michael turned to face Mr. Keeler. "Excuse me," Michael said. "This is a smoke-free festival. I'm sure you weren't aware."

Mr. Keeler blew out another mouthful of smoke. "I was aware."

Michael's cheeks turned red, and his back straightened. Dad patted him on the back. Then he turned to me and winked. That wink meant something, just a shared moment between Dad and me at Michael's expense.

Michael stood up, pulling away from Dad. "This is a family festival and—"

"Family festival." Mr. Keeler spat the words. "You're like all them other pansies out there, flitting around for free magnets and stickers. I remember when these festivals were about fighting. When we worried about whether or not the police were gonna haul us away, not whether or not we had face painting and balloon animals. Or cigarettes." He held the cigarette to his lips and took another long draw.

"Well," said Michael. "I just wanted you to be aware." He picked up his drink, turned to us. "Let's go somewhere a little cleaner," he said. He swept off, leaving Dad and me to follow his angry strides.

As we left the seating area, Dad nodded to Mr. Keeler and again said, "Happy Pride."

Mr. Keeler muttered the word, "Pansies." But he winked at me and gave me a tiny, half smile as I followed Dad. I smiled back. I couldn't help it.

Michael was halfway across the park before he settled on a clear patch of grass by one of the stages. He sat down and took a long sip of his lemonade, his shoulders still tight.

Finally he sighed. "Well."

The spot was shady. We listened to a woman singing ballads on the nearby stage.

"Now, this is nice," Dad said lying back, his

hands under his head.

"I need to tinkle," Michael said. "I'm feeling that first lemonade. I'll be back."

Michael ran off to the line of port-a-johns leaving Dad and me sitting in the grass.

"So," Dad said. "What do you think?"

"I think he has a small bladder," I said.

Dad laughed. "That's the truth. But I meant the festival."

I shrugged. "There aren't as many rainbows as I thought." I assumed from Michael's bin that the place would be like walking into a tub of Skittles.

I thought about Sage again. Was I really ashamed of Dad? Why was my first impulse to hide him? It was the same thing Mom always did. She never talked about Dad being bi. She said she wanted to give him a fair chance in people's mind. But was it really fair to hide who he was?

Before long, the stage turned over to a poet who talked about her experience growing up transgender and her journey from male to female. A few of her poems were sad, but most of them were funny and bright. I had never thought gender was something that could be hilarious. Maybe it takes someone who really knows it to find the humor in it.

Emily and Robi from Cocktail Hour came over to say hi. I sucked the melted ice out of my cup and watched people walking past. After I ate a couple of the chewy Real Foods bars, I saw Michael coming out of the crowd. He was carrying something.

When he walked up, Dad sat up. "Feel better?" Dad asked.

"Sorry it took so long," Michael said. "I made a detour to get you these." He held out baseball caps to Dad and me. "Since you two aren't into rainbows."

Mine was navy blue with the word ALLY stitched in crisp white. I looked up to see Michael removing Dad's Timberwolves cap, replacing it with one that had the blue, pink and purple bisexual flag on it.

"Thank you," Dad said before pecking Michael a kiss. "I mean it. This is just right."

I held the Ally cap in my hands, unsure. "Thanks," I said, tucking the hat into my bag with the empty granola bar wrappers.

I picked up my cup and sucked the last watery liquid from the bottom.

"I'm starving," Dad said. "Let's find some food."

After getting a pile of kabobs and fresh-cut fries, we went back to the picnic tables. Mr. Keeler was gone.

As the afternoon wore on, we finished the loop of booths and tables. Dad and I found a shady place under a large oak tree. Michael went to keep mingling. Dad lay down in the grass. It wasn't long before his breathing became steady. He was asleep.

I sat watching people walk past, families, boyfriends, girlfriends. So, this was my new world. I looked over at Dad's bi flag hat. There is no way he would have worn it last year. Maybe it was good for him to be here where he could wear whatever he wanted to.

As the sun shifted to the west, the crowd shifted, too. Many of the people with children were heading home. More adults were arriving. I had expected the festival to die down as the day wore on. Instead, the air became charged.

Michael returned. "We'll be bringing out the real bands soon," he said, looking up from a schedule. "Then we've got the fireworks."

As I kept watching the crowd, I saw Sage walking through the mass of people. Two women walked hand in hand beside her. They turned down the path that led out of the park. Sage and her moms.

"Be right back," I said to Dad and Michael. I bolted towards the three figures, catching up before Sage and her moms went too far.

"Hey," I said.

The three of them turned to me.

"Hi," Sage said. We just stared at each other

for a minute. The two women with her stared
at me, puzzled. They were both short. One
had long red hair that flowed down over her
shoulders, making her look sort of like a hippie.
The other looked like Sage, sharing her perfect
oval face shape, but her hair was short and she
wore a polo shirt and khaki shorts. Sage looked
extra bright contrasted against them.

"Are these your moms?" I asked.

"Yeah," Sage said, turning to them. "Moms,
meet Jeremiah, the bicycle boy."

The one with red hair extended her hand. "I'm
Reina."

"And I'm Lisa," said the one in the polo.
Sage pointed to Lisa. "She's the Hmong one."
Her moms laughed.

"Sage talks about you all the time," Lisa said.
I could feel my cheeks get warm.

"Do you want to meet my dad?" I asked them.
I took a deep breath. "And his boyfriend?"

Sage's face lit up. "Um, obviously."

I led them back into the crowd, then up onto

the grass to where Dad and Michael sat waiting. As I did, I pulled out my Ally cap, hesitating, not quite ready to put it on my head.

"I like it," Sage said, pointing to the cap.

I blushed, stuffing it into my bag once again as I made the introductions.

The next morning, we skipped church to go to the pride parade.

Michael left early. He was riding the Uni-cycle in the parade. Although he invited Dad and me to ride along, I passed. Dad said he would join me in the crowd to cheer.

While Dad showered, I sat with *The Grapes of Wrath*, trying to force myself through another chapter. I was actually relieved when my phone rang with a call from Mom.

"Jer Bear," she said. "What have you been up to?"

I told her about the festival and parade.

"That's been a long time coming," she said. "Your father never went to Pride with me."

"With you?" I asked. "Did you go by yourself?"

"No," Mom said. "I had a lot of lesbian friends in college."

I was surprised. "Oh."

"I miss you, Jer," Mom said. "Are you sure you want to stay there all summer?"

"Mom," I said, annoyed, "I'm staying here for the summer. I always do."

She sighed. "I know. But you're not trapped. It's not like we have court papers or mandates. If this system isn't working, we can do something different. You could go out for holidays or something."

Dad walked into the room, buckling his belt.

"I'm fine," I said into the phone. "I've got to go now."

"Okay Jer Bear," she said. "Love and hugs."

"Don't forget to water your tomatoes." I hung up the phone.

Dad smiled. "If they're still alive," he said, rolling his eyes.

In the alley behind our building, we ran into Sage and Reina. Her mom Lisa was marching in the parade with Hmong Pride. We joined them on the way to the parade, getting seats in the grandstand on Hennepin.

"We probably look like a normal family," I said to Sage.

Sage elbowed me. "Not normal," she said, "Just straight."

The parade opened with a bunch of women riding motorcycles led by the mayor of Minneapolis. Then came a rainbow flag as wide as the street, followed by other flags. The bi flag, a pink, blue and white one that Sage said was the trans flag, the leather flag, and several others. As the parade continued and floats went by, I dreaded the moment when Michael would ride past.

A group of people wearing matching T-shirts marched past with a Senator. A float for Marzetti's Hardware went by; several of Lisa's coworkers recognized Sage and Reina and threw us handfuls of taffy. Trucks pulled floats from real estate places and health clinics. Lisa marched past with the group from Hmong Pride, carrying their banner high.

As the parade was winding down, I saw the bicycles coming down the street, looping around the pavement. Everyone wore their pride. Some people were in drag. Several cyclists tied rainbow streamers to their handlebars. Even in the colorful mix, Michael and the Uni-cycle stuck out.

"Whoa!" Sage yelled to me. "Is that Michael?"

I could feel my face burning. "Yeah," I said.

Sage laughed. I was surprised that there was nothing mean in it. "I love his bike," she said. "I want one so bad."

Michael rode into the distance and people stood up. We followed the crowd and filled Hennepin Avenue with people as we marched back towards Loring Park. The parade was officially over, but somehow, I felt a part of it all.

We spent the afternoon in the park, eating cheese curds, corn dogs and more kabobs with Sage, Reina and Lisa. I still didn't like Michael. And he was still embarrassing. But at least he wasn't a secret any more.

CHAPTER

Days with Michael settled into a routine: I avoided him and he tried to pry into my life. It was never big stuff, just the little things. Always asking what I was doing, where I was going, when I would be back, reminding me to look out for potholes.

"Don't forget water," he told me after I said

I was going on a ride with Sage. He stood on a stool in the kitchen brushing paint into the corner where the roller would not be able to reach. The paint was bold yellow. When I complained about the lack of color with the "Hazelnut Cream" walls, I didn't mean to make the kitchen look like a tub of mustard.

"When are you going to be home?" he said.

"Later." I said. "Before supper."

I turned again to go. "Jer," he called. I stiffened at the nickname. Only my parents could call me that.

"I'm Jeremiah," I said.

Michael turned a little red. "Jeremiah, I feel like you're avoiding me. I know I'm not your dad, but I really hope you'll give me a chance. I've never been anyone's parent, and I'm new at this."

I looked up at Michael, perched on top of his ladder in his white painting costume. Even when he was painting, his hair was still perfect.

"Don't worry," I said, a well of annoyance

building up inside of me. "You'll never have to be my dad."

Even as I left the apartment, I felt a little bad about it. But it was better to be clear, right? I remembered what Mr. Keeler said. If I didn't get rid of Michael now, I could be stuck with him forever.

I got my bike and met Sage in the alley.

I sighed.

"What?" she asked, looking at the scowl on my face.

"Michael," I said.

She laughed. Something had changed after Pride. I couldn't quite explain it, but Sage and I were more connected. Maybe it was the knowledge neither of us needed to keep secrets from the other person.

Every day we had explored, riding a little further than the last. Soon I knew more than how to get to the library. Sage showed me where to buy popsicles, the "secret" path across the highway, and a building that looked like a castle. Sometimes we rode to Marzetti's for free popcorn when Lisa was working.

"We're going somewhere new today." Sage's eyes opened wide with excitement. "I've been saving it. It's my favorite place. It's like a temple."

"Ok," I said. I didn't know what to expect. Going to church was enough religion. I didn't know how I felt about temples.

The ride was surprisingly short. We came to a park full of oaks. A massive building rose through the screen of trees. It looked like a Greek temple with the huge stone pillars. I had passed the building several times, but hadn't bothered about it. It looked so official I had assumed it was probably a government building.

"It's the MIA," Sage said, her voice full of excitement. "The Minneapolis Institute of the Arts, but they call it Mia. There are rooms and rooms of pure beauty. You'll love it."

"An art museum?" I asked. Going to an art museum wasn't nearly as intimidating as a temple.

Sage giggled. "You always think so boring," she said.

As Sage pulled me through the galleries, I thought maybe there was something to her temple theory. Somehow, it did feel holy in here, kind of like a church.

People moved slowly, quietly, and stood before paintings and sculptures.

Sage led me through halls of marble statues, up a flight of stairs, through a room filled with menorahs and six-pointed stars. We came to a gallery filled with large paintings, some of them abstract. I didn't know much about art, but I knew these were newer in the broad sense.

Finally, with a dramatic sigh, Sage dropped onto a bench in front of the largest painting in the room. The canvas was as big as the wall. It was unlike any painting I had seen before.

"This," said Sage, "this is the painting that I come to see. It's beautiful. It's magic."

I rolled my eyes, but as I sat beside her and

stared, I realized she was right. There was a sense of movement in the painting that I hadn't seen in any other. People were posing in various ways on the canvas, a grandmother, a woman by a wood stove. In the center, a nude woman stood, arms outstretched in some sort of victorious moment, almost like the boxer, Rocky.

Normally, nudes made me embarrassed, but there was something about this woman, so bold as she stared out from her painting, that I didn't feel embarrassed at all. It was like she was daring me to do something, something as bold and reckless as she was doing.

I turned. Sage was standing beside in the same victorious pose, arms high over her head. I looked around, several people were staring. I felt my cheeks get hot.

I walked away from her to read the plaque. "*The Studio* by Larry Rivers, oil on canvas." It amazed me how something so big could be labeled with just a few, simple words.

I returned to Sage who was sitting now. We

stared at the painting a long time. "It makes me want to do something," Sage said. Her voice was low and reverent.

"Yeah," I said. The woman in the painting stood there, not hiding anything, bold and unafraid. "Me, too."

After that, we wandered through more of the museum. Gallery opened to gallery.

It wasn't long before I checked the time and realized we had spent the entire afternoon lost in the labyrinth of art.

On the ride back to the apartment, Sage was unusually quiet. Finally, she spoke. "What are we going to do?"

"What do you mean?" I asked.

"What we were saying," she said, "is that we need to do something. Something bold." She let go of her handlebars and shot her arms into the air for a microsecond. "Something that makes us do this inside."

I laughed. "Can we keep our clothes on, though?"

Sage smiled. "We've just got to do something."

I don't know that much about art. I don't know what the artist meant in the painting, but I think one of the points may have been that the woman did have to be naked. I don't mean like really naked. But she was there. Just herself in the middle of all this ordinary stuff.

She was being herself.

CHAPTER

8

"**You should come over** to my apartment,"
Sage said. "You shouldn't have to be by
yourself."

I had just told her about Cocktail Hour. We
were lying on our backs in the park. She was
naming more clouds. Emile and Georgie.

I shrugged. "I don't mind."

"I never get to have friends over," she said. "And if we're having company, we could probably have ice cream."

So it was that when Dad and Michael headed out to Big Ben and Little Jon's place, I followed Sage into the building next door.

It was pretty much like our building. It must have been built during the same time. The main difference was that the floors of their hall were scuffed up old wood instead of the floors that Michael called "terrazzo" in our hallways.

I followed her into her apartment on the second floor. It looked out over the parking lot towards our building. Lisa stood in the kitchen, still in her uniform from Marzetti's Hardware.

"Want something to drink?" Lisa asked.

She poured Sage and me tall glasses of lemonade. I could tell it was the powdered stuff from a canister. It tasted like home.

We sat at the table. Reina joined us. She had a dandelion woven into her long braid, and wore a crystal pendant around her neck.

After the lemonade, Sage took me to her room. Their apartment was the same layout as ours, mirror image, but she had the room closer to the bathroom, like Dad and Michael. I looked over the pictures hanging in the hall. There were several baby pictures, newborn Sage with her moms holding her between them.

One picture was of the family at the hospital, Sage in Lisa's arms, Lisa wearing a hospital gown, her face puffy and splotched. Reina sat next to them, beaming.

Sage walked back next to me to look at the picture.

"Yeah," she said. "That's the day I was born."

I tried to wrap my mind around it. "You weren't adopted?"

"No," she said. "Why?"

I shrugged. "I guess I just assumed since you have two moms and all…" My face turned red when I saw the look of annoyance on her face. "Sorry," I said. I guess it made sense. Sage did look like Lisa. But where did she get her crazy, frizzy curls?

Sage sighed. "A lot of people assume I was adopted. It's no big deal."

I followed her into her bedroom. "My mom conceived me through A.I." Sage said.

"A.I.?" I said. More letters I didn't understand.

"Artificial Insemination," she said. I could feel my cheeks turning pink. She said the words like it was no big deal. Something normal.

"I never met the sperm donor," she said. "My moms have information about him, but I don't really see the point right now. He gave me the curls and green eyes. And gave me life on some level, obviously. But he's not really like a dad or something."

I nodded, hoping that was the right response. I took the pause to look around her room. Her bedspread was magenta, heaped with pillows of all shapes and sizes, including a large pink frog and a giant cushy cupcake. Just about what I would have expected.

Photographs covered the walls. They weren't framed or anything, just stuck into the plaster with thumb tacks. They weren't in any particular order, but I could pick out Sage in most of them, growing up from a bald baby to a girl with the giant head of hair.

When I looked at Sage, she was smiling again.

"That's my life," she said. "All over those walls."

She started pointing to pictures and telling stories. There was a picture of her at Hmong New Year dressed in what Sage said was traditional Hmong clothing, standing next to her similarly garbed grandmother, pictures of her with Lisa and Reina holding signs at demonstrations for the right to marry, pictures of school events and festivals. In most of the photos, Sage was sandwiched between Lisa and Reina.

I had pictures like this from my early childhood, squished between Mom and Dad. Now all of my pictures had an empty space next to me.

"Your moms have always been together?" I asked. I sat down on a purple beanbag chair and looked up. She had white paper clouds cut out in all shapes and sizes attached to her ceiling.

"Not always," Sage said, laughing. "But since before I was born, yeah."

Lisa poked her head into the bedroom. "The ice cream isn't going to eat itself," she said.

We followed Lisa into the dining room where Reina sat at the table, brushing clear stuff onto a bunch of little disks.

"Prepping for the Red Hot Art Fest," Reina said. "This year, we just went for it and got a table. They're more craft than art, but still." She held up the tray. They had taken clippings from old comic books and turned the vintage superheroes into pendants, keychains, medallions, and pins.

"They're cool," I said, picking up a keychain that said, KA-POW!!!!!.

Reina pushed the pendants aside to make

room for the dishes of ice cream Lisa was passing around. It was soft and sweet in the lingering heat.

That night before bed, I called Mom. I told her about visiting Sage and her moms.

"You have a friend." Mom sounded happy. "I've been hoping you wouldn't stay cooped up with a couple of old fogies for the whole summer. Or one of your old books. Dead white men."

"I read classics," I said, hardly thinking that Dad and Michael deserved to be called old fogies.

"I should make you a list of some more diverse authors," Mom said.

"Yeah," I agreed. She often said this. She never did.

"If you have a friend you can make it through just about anything," Mom said.

I wondered about her. Sure, she had friends that came and went. The occasional person from her art studio or yoga class. Still, I thought she was probably lonely, especially when I wasn't there during the summer.

I thought about all the pictures of Sage pressed between her parents. About Lisa and Reina working on their pendants together.

"What about you?" I asked her. "Do you have someone?"

"I have my art," Mom said breezily. "My art and my work."

"Don't you ever wish you had someone?" Every now and again I tested the waters, hanging onto a thin line of hope that my parents could reunite someday.

"Men get in the way," Mom said. "I don't need a relationship like that."

I wondered whether it was true.

"Guess what?" Mom asked. "I watered the tomatoes this morning."

CHAPTER

"You should meet Mr. Keeler," I said
to Sage the next morning. I was waiting on the
stoop to help him water the Potentilla Fruticosa.
I knew he would be down soon.

Sage stood in front of me, biting her lip.

Suddenly the door to the building opened and
out he walked. Sage stared up at him, her eyes

wide.

"What?" Mr. Keeler asked, "You've never seen a wrinkled old cur before?"

I stood up. "Mr. Keeler, this is Sage. Sage, Mr. Keeler."

"Hello," Sage said in a small voice.

"I've seen her," Mr. Keeler growled, reaching out his shaky arm to hand me the watering can. "You cut one of my shrubs."

"I didn't know it was yours," Sage said, her voice gathering strength. "I didn't know anyone cared about these bushes."

"Now you know." Mr. Keeler sat down on the stoop, fishing a cigarette out of his shirt pocket. I watched them out of the corner of my eye as I filled the can and started watering. Sage stared at Mr. Keeler, then at me. I smiled at her.

She took a deep breath. "It's a very nice garden," Sage said hopefully. I nodded at her, trying to encourage her.

Mr. Keeler huffed. "It's a pile of rocks. It used to be full of lilies. Bright orange ones. Daylilies.

Hemerocallis."

"I know what Hemerocallis is," Sage said. "There was a whole bed of daylilies behind my old house. They used to bloom all summer. Once, when I was little, I picked one and cried and cried when it wilted after just one day."

Mr. Keeler huffed, but didn't say anything as he finished his cigarette. He flicked his cigarette butt out into the sidewalk, then took the empty watering can back from me.

Sage and I watched him walk back up into the building. When the door slammed shut behind him, I turned to Sage.

"He's not so bad, is he?" I asked.

"He's kind of like this garden," she said. "Rocky, but with a chance of finding good soil underneath."

"I guess," I said.

"He likes daylilies," she added. "I think I could like him."

We sat side by side on the steps. "I was thinking," I said. The idea had just occurred to me. I hesitated, then spat it out. "It might be interesting to plant flowers in here in front of the building. Daylilies. Or something. For Mr. Keeler. As a surprise." My hands ached with the desire to work through the soil.

Sage stood up. "Please, please, please," she said. "I can picture it now, full of a wild tangle of lilies blooming all summer."

"Something like that," I said.

At lunch, I brought up the idea with Michael. "I was thinking we might try to plant something in front of the building."

Michael dropped his fork. His cheeks were slightly pink, and he was smiling. "Wow," he said. "I mean yes. Yes. We should check in with Maxine. She's probably in the office today. Let's go now."

"Now?" I said. I hadn't thought about the details, getting everything approved and all that. The idea suddenly seemed daunting.

Michael stood up. "It's absolutely no problem. Let's catch her before she is out for the afternoon."

As I followed him down the stairs, I couldn't help but be impressed by his eagerness to help.

"Thanks so much for thinking of this," Michael said. "I have always been interested in organic gardening. We could do some native plants or something."

We? He wanted to do this, too? Then it hit me. I had said we might try to plant. I meant Sage and me. He thought I meant *we* as *him and me*.

Suddenly we were standing in the arctic air-conditioning of Maxine's office. I was telling her the idea. She stared at us behind red-framed eye glasses.

"Of course all the labor would be free," Michael added.

"Oh!" she exclaimed, smiling at us. "Well, why not. If you do the work, you can do whatever you want, and I say screw the management. I probably have a few dollars somewhere to help get a couple of plants."

She began rummaging around in her desk.

"We can get that later," Michael said. "Thank you."

I followed him out of the office. He led the way outside to stand in front of the garden. I couldn't bring myself to tell him it was a mistake; I didn't want or need his help.

I should've just let it go. Michael was so excited. It probably wouldn't hurt to have the extra help. At least until the rocks were out of the way.

"What's the plan?" Michael asked, waving his hand over the rocky bed.

Just then, Mr. Keeler opened the door. Michael's shoulders tightened when he saw his nemesis.

Mr. Keeler sat down, breathing hard from walking down the stairs. The cigarette in his mouth was almost spent even though smoking was against the rules in the building. He glared at Michael.

"What are you so excited about?" Mr. Keeler

asked. He blew out a mouthful of smoke.

"We're making this wasteland into a garden," Michael said. "I don't think anyone will be sad to see these mangy shrubs go."

Mr. Keeler pulled the cigarette from his mouth. "Those are Potentilla Fruticosa. You'll take those over my dead body. Those bushes have been here almost as long as I have. I watered them out of my own faucet during the drought of '92. You think you can tear out anything, you young people. Just because it's old."

Michael wasn't looking up at Mr. Keeler anymore. I hadn't had the chance to tell Michael the whole plan, planting lilies around the bushes. And I hadn't told him it was supposed to be a surprise for Mr. Keeler.

"We're keeping the bushes," I said. "They just need some company."

Mr. Keeler ground the end of his cigarette into the stoop, then flicked his cigarette butt onto the sidewalk. "Damn straight," he said.

"We have a receptacle for your cigarette

butts," Michael said.

Mr. Keeler didn't look at him as he stood up and walked back inside.

As the door slammed shut, Michael growled. "That man. He drives me crazy." Michael took a deep breath, picked the cigarette butt off the sidewalk, and dropped it into the coffee can.

"Well," said Michael, putting his hand on my shoulder. "I'm yours to command. Should we start now?"

"No," I said. "We'll get to it."

Michael looked disappointed. "There's no time like the present. I can't wait to help."

So far, he hadn't been any help at all. "We'll start later," I said. Michael's face fell as I turned and stomped back into the building.

As we ate our free-range chicken salad for supper, Michael told Dad about the plan to put in a garden.

Dad smiled. "It sounds like exactly what you two need," he said.

"Yeah," I said. Dad looked so happy about it.

I really tried to sound enthusiastic.

Dad cleared his throat, "You know, Jer," he said. "I was thinking we could have a day out tomorrow, just you and me."

"Really?" I said. "Okay."

"It's the Fourth of July." Michael said. "I thought we could get the garden started. And have a picnic or something."

"You have all summer," Dad said. "Jer and I usually go fishing on the Fourth. We'll try to bring back something for dinner."

"When were you going to inform me of this holiday tradition?" Michael asked.

Dad shrugged. "I just did."

Michael sighed. "Well, if you're going fishing, I am going on the Freedom from Pants Ride."

"The what?" I asked, hoping I hadn't heard right.

Michael laughed. "It's just a thing we do in Minneapolis. Every Fourth of July, a group meets across the street in Stevens Square and takes a bike ride through the city. Sans pants."

I'm pretty sure that means without pants! I was suddenly even more thankful that I was about to spend the day fishing with Dad.

Michael eyed Dad. "Be back in time for fireworks. They start at dusk and we'll need some time to find a place down at the river. I wish I would have known. I could have bought some better fishing food for the two of you."

"Don't worry," Dad said. "I've got it covered."

Michael smiled. "What does that mean—that you're going to Subway?"

Dad shrugged. "We'll figure something out."

Fishing. A whole day with Dad. A whole day without Michael.

CHAPTER

10

It was still dark when Dad and I woke
up to go fishing. Dad had gathered what we
needed the night before so we could make a fast
getaway. But it wasn't fast enough.

"Make sure you bring enough water," Michael
said, yawning. He stood in the living room in
his boxer briefs and undershirt. I had never seen

him up so early. He was the type of person who made sure he got his beauty sleep. "You're sure you don't want me to throw together a lunch?"

Dad pointed to the cooler. "I got it."

Michael raised his eyebrow. "I'm impressed. Don't forget sunscreen."

"I got it." Dad walked over to Michael and squeezed him in a hug. "We'll be home in time for fireworks tonight."

Just as we picked up our fishing poles, Michael spoke again. "You'll want hats," he said. "It gets bright on the water."

"Good thinking," Dad said. Dad pulled a hat on. At first I thought it was the Timberwolves cap he always wore, but Michael was smiling at Dad. I now realized Dad was wearing the bisexual flag hat that Michael bought at the festival.

"I'm fine," I said.

Dad shrugged. "It does get pretty bright out there."

I went back to my room. The Ally cap was still

sitting on my dresser. I grabbed my sunglasses instead.

I walked back to the front door. "I'm ready," I said, making sure to let Michael see that I carried sunglasses instead of that hat.

Finally, we were out the door.

On the way down the stairs, Dad handed me the cooler. It was light. I opened the lid.

"Shouldn't there be food in here?" I asked Dad.

He winked at me. "There will be."

We stopped at the gas station and Dad bought a large bag of ice, two Mountain Dews, two "Monster" subs, a carton of donuts, and a pair of coffees. I didn't usually like coffee, but it was a special occasion.

The sky began to glow dimly as we drove east to Stillwater, evidently Dad's favorite fishing place out here.

We pulled up to a park with a long pier that jutted out into the river.

"This spot will probably be full of picnickers

later," Dad said. "Hopefully, we'll catch a few before the crowd."

The St. Croix River stretched out in front of us. It was about the width of the Mississippi in Minneapolis. Probably, they met up somewhere and became the same river. The water was completely silent, even the lapping at the pier where we sat couldn't be heard over the rustle of leaves in the breeze.

It was just Dad and me. Just like old times before Michael was there always filling the space between us with chatter. We didn't even have to think about him.

We slowly got our poles ready and hooks baited.

Dad opened the carton of powdered-sugar donuts. "What Michael doesn't know won't hurt him," he said, winking at me.

Not even ten minutes on the pier and we already referenced Michael. I sighed and picked up a donut. The bitter coffee was actually okay as long as you drank between bites of the donut. I brushed the powdered sugar from my fingertips.

I cast my line into the deep water, reeling it back slowly as the river carried it downstream. Fishing on a river was more active than fishing on a lake. Dad and I had to pay attention so our lines didn't tangle. Soon we had a rhythm down. We didn't have to say anything. It just was.

The silence was full around us.

Several joggers passed. The breeze picked up, driving clouds across the sky. I wondered if Sage was naming them back in Stevens Square.

"Think we'll get any rain?" I asked, surprised at my need for some noise.

Dad looked up at the sky. "It'll hold off." He picked up another donut.

When the box was half empty, Dad reeled in his line and paused. "You having a nice summer?"

I shrugged. "Yeah."

Dad held his fishing pole still, staring out at the river. I watched as my bobber floated along in the deep water.

Finally, Dad cast his line again and cleared his throat. "What do you think of Michael? Really think of him?" His voice was measured, like he was testing.

So there it was. Michael. Again. "He's okay." I cast my line back out.

Dad smiled. "You think so?"

I hesitated. "He's different. Different from you."

Dad brought in his line and slowly replaced the worm with one that still had life in it. "He's different?" Dad cast again, his bobber moving slowly with the current.

I tried to formulate what I wanted to say. Something about the Uni-cycle, the highlighted hair, the painting clothes, the reminders to bring water and avoid potholes.

Just then, there was a tug on Dad's line. He pulled in a bluegill. It flopped in the air as Dad pulled it from the water. It was too small. Dad's big hands held it still while I removed the hook.

"Independence Day," Dad said. "Swim free, little guy." He reached down and let the fish squirm away into the murky shallows.

We sat there for a long time then, just the two of us. I weighed whether or not I wanted to bring Michael up again. I decided it was lucky he was out of the picture for the present.

The sky cleared. I put on my sunglasses.

Eventually, Dad brought out the Mountain Dew and the subs. It wasn't noon yet, but we had been up since before dawn. We ate on the pier next to our fishing poles. The soda was sweet and thick.

When we finished our lunch, Dad suggested we take a break. We carried our poles, cooler, and tackle box to the shade of a maple. Dad lay back and was out like a light. I couldn't understand how he could do that so easily, especially just after downing a Mountain Dew.

I thought about his question, *What do you think about Michael?* His voice was so controlled when he asked, that I knew he must really care about it. I wondered what he thought about Michael. I was afraid I already knew, but I needed to know for sure.

I lay beside Dad, watching the river, listening to the breeze in the leaves above me.

The shrieks of kids on the nearby playground woke me up. Dad was sitting up. When he saw me awake, he looked down at his watch.

"Well," he said. "I think the fish won today. I guess that means I don't have to bother cleaning anything. We should probably head home."

We packed up the gear. As we drove down the highway, I took a deep breath, then asked the question. "Dad, what do you think about Michael?"

"Well," Dad scratched behind his ear, which had turned pink. "I like him." He continued to stare straight ahead at the highway, but a smile crept onto his face and his cheeks turned a little pink. "I like him a lot."

"Yeah?"

Dad looked at me for just a moment before

turning back to the highway. "A whole lot."

I took a deep breath and let out a long sigh.

I could tell Dad was looking at me, but I was looking straight ahead at the highway.

"Dad," I said after a while. "I think Michael is annoying. Sometimes."

Dad actually laughed out loud. "Fair enough, Jer." Dad patted me on the back. "Fair enough."

When we got home, a large cutting board was on the dining room table. A filet knife sat on top, ready to use. Apparently, Michael had great faith in us.

Michael hurried in. Thankfully he was in shorts again after his freedom-from-pants bike ride.

"So," he said, gesturing towards the cooler. "Make a good haul?"

I shook my head, but Dad just smiled big. "Well, we caught so many we sold them all to Brit's Pub. They said they'd fry 'em up for us."

Michael rolled his eyes, but laughed. "We shouldn't keep them waiting. Wash up and we can go. I'm starving. Nothing builds an appetite like riding a bike in underwear."

After stuffing ourselves with fish and chips at Brit's Pub, we went back to the apartment for our bikes. I cringed as the Uni-cycle rattled up the stairs behind me. When we all got out to the alley, I tried to prepare myself for another ride with the unicorn behind me with that huge, creepy grin.

I looked away.

"Watch out for potholes," Michael called as we rode down the alley. The sidewalks were full of people walking towards the river. Michael got catcalled just as much as the last time. This time, the streets were full enough that I didn't feel quite so tied to him. Still, my cheeks were hot as I pedaled.

By the time we got to the Mississippi, the waterfront was already crowded. Children ran between picnic blankets. Finally, Michael pointed to an empty space in a patch of long grass.

"Looks as good as any," Dad said. Apparently, the spot was abandoned for a reason: the grass turned out to be old weeds, pokey and stiff. Dad stomped his heavy boots to force them down. Michael unrolled a rainbow picnic blanket.

We all sat down, Dad between Michael and me, connecting us and thankfully separating us too. As the fireworks ignited, the river reflected the explosions of light. I kept looking at Dad and Michael, the light reflecting in their eyes. Michael leaned against Dad's side. Dad liked him a lot. A whole lot.

CHAPTER

Sunday morning, on the way home
from Open Arms, I paused at the rocky beds
in front of our building. That morning Pastor
Veronica had preached about blooming where
God plants us. I stared at the lonely bushes and
dry rocks, waiting patiently. We needed to start
it soon; it was already so late in the season. But

that meant working with Michael.

"We could start clearing rocks this afternoon," Michael said, pausing with Dad at the front door before going inside.

The sun was already beating down. Dad had said that this was forecast to be one of the hottest weeks of the summer.

We should start, but I shook my head.

"It's too hot today," I said. I was beginning to wonder whether this garden business was worth the trouble. "It's not good for plants to be transplanted during really hot times."

Dad slapped me on the back. "That's the truth," he said. "It's not good for people, either."

When we entered our apartment, it was hot. Dad walked around closing the blinds halfway to reduce the amount of sunlight streaming in.

"Where did this heat come from?" Dad asked after lunch as he dropped onto the sofa. "Even the couch is hot. Let's get out of here. The lake. You wanna go to the lake?"

I smiled, excited to do something.

Dad heaved himself off the couch and pulled his shirt back on. "Alright, troops, let's go." He walked towards the door and grabbed his keys.

"Don't we need our swimming suits?" I asked.

"Heck," he said. "My clothes could use a little freshening up."

I laughed.

"Michael," Dad said. "Let's get out of here."

I could feel my shoulders tighten.

"Allen, could you at least wait until I finish washing the dishes?" Michael said. "Give me fifteen minutes and then we can head out."

"Michael," Dad said, "Leave 'em. Dishes don't melt as easily as humans."

Michael dried his hands and put them on his hips. "Fifteen minutes."

"Sir," Dad said. "I am going to have to ask you to exit the kitchen. I repeat. Exit the kitchen."

Michael laughed. "Fine," he said, pulling off his dishwashing gloves. "Give me a minute to change."

"What for?" Dad asked.

Michael raised his eyebrows. "Do you know how much I spent on these shorts? There is no way I would get them sandy."

He went to the bedroom. There was now enough time for me to get into my swimsuit, but I looked at Dad's annoyed, settled, expression and decided I would go in my cut-off jeans, like him.

Michael came out several minutes later in bright red shorts that barely reached the middle of his thigh and fit him close. He had three towels with him. He handed one to me and one to Dad.

"We at least need towels," he said. "And let me grab some water."

Dad sighed. "You take good care of us."

As Michael walked into the kitchen for the water, Dad spun his towel and used it to snap Michael's butt. They both laughed.

Finally, we got out the door.

We rode the bus to Lake Bde Maka Ska. I took the seat next to Dad, forcing Michael to take the spot behind us. Riding in the air-conditioned bus made the trip already worth it. When we got off the bus at the lake, heat blasted us.

It looked like Lake Bde Maka Ska was the place to be. The beach was crowded, mostly with adults lying in the sun. The water was full of little kids.

Dad pulled off his sneakers and threw his keys and wallet inside. We ripped off our shirts. I was super white.

"I should have brought sunscreen," Michael said.

"I'm fine," I said.

"Race you," Dad said as soon as my shoes were off. He tore off down the beach. I followed him. Dad and I splashed into the water. It was wonderfully cold. Dad whooped like a little kid.

We plowed on until it was deep enough that Dad threw himself forward and plunged under the water. I did the same. The cool washed over me, dissolving the layer of sweat.

I came up before he did. He could hold his breath forever. Finally, he came up spouting water out of his mouth.

Michael waded through the water towards us. He was painfully slow, trying to adjust to the water little by little. Dad ran at him and tackled him into the waves. Michael came up screaming. The lifeguard yelled something about "no horseplay."

Dad led Michael out to the deep water where I was. We floated, letting the water hold us. Dad took the opportunity to dunk Michael several more times when the lifeguard wasn't looking. Although Michael protested and put up a fight, he always came up smiling.

When we were thoroughly cooled down, we went back to our towels and shoes. As we sat in the sun, letting the water evaporate from our bodies, I looked at Michael. His hair was stringy from the water, sticking out at odd angles. It made him look just a little bit less plastic.

I almost felt that I was getting used to him for a minute. Then he handed me a water bottle and told me to stay hydrated.

"And you should probably cover your shoulders so you don't burn," he added.

CHAPTER

(12)

I looked up from reading another chapter
of *The Grapes of Wrath* on the stoop. A block
away, Mr. Keeler hobbled slowly down the
sidewalk towards our building. He seemed
fragile, tottering along, putting each foot
deliberately in front of the other. His arm was
low, carrying a single plastic bag.

I stood up and walked over to him. "You want any help?"

He eyed me. "Help? You gonna take my bag and run? You think I couldn't chase you?"

"I'm not trying to take anything," I said, even though we both already knew it was true. I walked with him until we reached the front steps.

He stood, catching his breath.

"You haven't done much," he said, nodding at the garden.

"We're still planning," I said. I was still avoiding the project, not wanting to have to face working with Michael.

"Alright then," Mr. Keeler said, holding the bag out to me. I took it. It was lighter than I expected from the way he held it, a box of cereal and a few cans. I followed his slow steps up the stairs. He lived on the second floor.

When we got to his apartment, I handed him the bag. He closed the door without so much as a thank you.

For some reason, I told Michael about it during our lunch of steamed organic "vegetable medley."

Michael shook his head. "I knew this day would come. God is trying to get even with me. She always does. I thought I had gotten out of this."

"What do you mean?" I asked.

"You know how I feel about Mr. Keeler," said Michael. "And now I have to buy him groceries. It's not the first time, but I swore I'd never do it again. He obviously can't get further than the corner store. Cereal. And I bet that canned soup is overloaded with sodium. We'll pick up a few things for him this afternoon."

"Okay," I said. I didn't understand why Michael would do this for Mr. Keeler, the man who drove him crazy.

Pretty soon, Michael and I were walking down the street towards Real Foods. He bribed me with the promise of a soda if I came along, but I would have come anyways. I was curious.

Michael led the way up and down the aisles at Real Foods acting as tour guide. He swept his hand over the shelves of food. "Of course, everything here is organic, so we don't have to watch for that. Soup. Low sodium soup seems a good thing when you're old. And probably prunes. Aisle six, on the left, midway, bottom shelf."

We passed several employees in teal aprons. Michael greeted each of them by name.

After filling a basket with all kinds of options, Michael led me to the refrigerator case full of soda. We stood before the glass bottles.

Instead of things like Fanta or Pepsi, the bottles had names and flavors I hadn't heard of. Juniper Berry, Clove & Grapefruit, Dandelion & Burdock. Michael confidently plucked a kombucha from the mix. Not wanting to seem indecisive, I grabbed a rhubarb soda.

A woman named Nissy rang us up at the register. As she filled the canvas bags that Michael had brought with him, she eyed me.

"You must be that Jeremiah kid," Nissy said.

"Yeah," I said. "How did you know?"

Nissy laughed. "You kidding me? Michael is always talking about you, trying to figure out how to be your friend."

I looked over at Michael who was now the color of the roasted red pepper tomato soup.

Nissy leaned in toward me, whispering extra loud so Michael could hear it. "Do us all a favor and just be his friend. He's a good guy."

Michael snatched the receipt from her. "Thank you, Nissy."

I followed him out of the store. He was breathing fast, refusing to make eye contact.

Apparently, Michael talked about me at work. I guess he was trying hard.

"Well." Michael spoke like he was trying to put the conversation with Nissy behind us. "Well. Now you've seen Real Foods."

"Yeah." I took a sip of my soda. It was light and bitter. I liked it.

When we got back to the apartment building,

we walked past the barren rocks, up the front steps. Michael led the way to Mr. Keeler's apartment.

Michael sighed. "Mr. Keeler's health is up and down. Some months, he just can't handle these stairs."

At Mr. Keeler's door, Michael knocked three times, quick and sharp.

The raspy voice of Mr. Keeler answered. "What?"

"Grocery delivery," Michael called back. Michael tried the doorknob. It was unlocked. He poked his head in the door. "Hello, Mr. Keeler."

I followed Michael into the apartment. It was sparse inside. The furniture was old. Mr. Keeler sat on a faded plaid sofa. He wore no shirt. The skin on his chest sagged, going up and down with his breathing.

Michael immediately moved to the cupboards and began unpacking.

Mr. Keeler huffed as he watched Michael. "I hope it's not any more of that organic shit."

"Mr. Keeler," Michael said in a stern voice. "Language."

Michael nodded significantly towards me. I realized he was trying to be parental, not letting other people swear in front of me.

Mr. Keeler huffed. "What? Don't swear in front of the kid?" He reached out a long arm, pointing at me. "Kids are tough. I wasn't much more than a kid when I was fighting at Stonewall. Do you think I cared when someone yelled a few cuss words?"

Michael pursed his lips. "I'm sure you didn't."

Mr. Keeler leaned back in his chair. "We were fighters then. Not like any of these rainbow pansies you see prancing around now." He shot Michael a look.

Michael forced a smile. "Would you like a glass of prune juice?"

"I could use a scotch on the rocks."

Michael walked forward, sliding his business card on the table. "Well, call if you need anything."

Mr. Keeler picked up the card and tossed it at the garbage can. It missed.

Michael rolled his eyes, then finished unpacking the groceries.

"Get some rest," Michael said.

Mr. Keeler gave a short laugh. "Rest? I can't do anything besides rest. Now get out."

I followed Michael into the hall.

"And that," said Michael through clenched teeth, "is why I can't stand Mr. Keeler."

We had just bought this man groceries and he did nothing besides insult Michael. And I could only guess it was the same way for Michael before.

I didn't get it. "Why do you help him, then?"

Michael laughed drily. "Perhaps I'm a glutton for punishment."

CHAPTER

Sage and I rode to the library again.
I was more thankful than ever for the air-
conditioning there. A librarian helped me locate
several new books on gardening. As Sage did
her usual ritual of reading odd pages from a tall
stack of books, I read tips on starting a garden.
I had maintained gardens, but starting them was

new to me. Soon, I had a clear vision of what needed to happen.

It was going to be more work than I had originally thought. I had the idea that it would just require clearing away a few rocks and slipping some daylilies into the ground. This book said I should be clearing and aerating a spot at least twice the diameter of the plant's pot. That didn't sound too bad until I realized that twice the diameter meant a spot over four times as big. If I wanted to plant a good-sized eight inch pot, it was going to need space the size of a trash can lid. For each plant.

The next morning, I led the way down the stairs, Michael bobbing along behind. Sage joined us on the stoop. The morning sun was already bright and hot.

I gave orders, explaining and outlining the eight places where we would strip away the rocks and plastic to make way for the daylilies. To my surprise, Michael stood by what he said: I was in charge.

I marked where each of the eight plants would go, and then we started. Sage and I worked side by side, scraping rocks out of the way. The rocks were jagged. They seemed to want to stay settled.

After a while, Sage went into her apartment and brought out two trowels. They weren't much help. Their blades caught between the rocks and sounded like someone's nails on a chalkboard. We went back to using our hands.

Michael worked on clearing the patch next to ours. The way he squatted, I assumed he was probably trying to keep his jeans clean. He plucked and picked out the rocks, taking tiny careful little handfuls and tossing them aside.

As our clear circles grew, I realized we hadn't been tossing our rocks far enough away, and we had to move a lot of them a second time to get the full 16 inch diameter. At last, we had a full circle of black plastic. I pulled out my pocket knife and cut away the plastic. The earth beneath was hard, packed down for years, unable to breathe. We joined Michael until his patch was cleared as well.

The circles of earth looked naked. But it wasn't an emptiness like the rocks. It was more like a blank canvas.

"Two down, six to go," Michael said.

Sage knelt down, resting her hand on the newly exposed earth. "It feels so hopeful," she said.

"It feels sweaty more than hopeful at this point," I said. The sun was climbing in the sky. When I said we'd done enough for the day, Michael looked relieved and went upstairs to clean up.

Sage and I rinsed away the dirt and dust under the spigot, then walked across the street to the park. We laid back on the grass in the shade of a large oak tree. I told her about me and Michael buying groceries for Mr. Keeler.

"But Michael says that he can't stand Mr. Keeler," I finished.

Sage squinted up at the sky. "Maybe he

actually likes Mr. Keeler a little. Not like romantic or anything. But, like maybe a father-figure or something?"

"Weird." I pulled a handful of grass and tossed it into the air. There was no breeze to carry it.

"Think about it," she said. "It might just be a little bit. But he buys Mr. Keeler groceries. And he's doing this garden for him."

I was about to say that he wasn't. That in fact, he was doing it for me, but the reality of that made me feel uncomfortable. Instead, I explained the whole mess of saying "we" to Michael and how Michael had been trying to do projects with me all summer.

"And you're sure you hate Michael?" Sage asked.

"Yeah," I said. "At least, I *was* sure. And I don't like changing my mind."

For the next several days, I avoided working in the garden. The heat and humidity gave me an easy out. Sage and I spent days at the library, soaking in the air conditioning.

At night, it would cool just enough for Dad and me to go out. We watched a movie in the park across the street. We went on another sweaty ride down the Greenway, passing the place where Dad and Michael met. We continued on the Greenway down to the Lake of the Isles. It didn't have beaches like Lake Bde Maka Ska, but it had a lot of trees that cast cool shade over the bike trail.

We parked our bikes and sat in a pool of shade.

"How's that garden shaping up?" Dad asked.

"We're taking it easy this week," I said. "Heat wave and all."

"You like working with Michael?" Dad's voice was level as he said this, but I could hear the edge of hope to it.

"It's okay." I picked up a rock and tossed it into the lake.

"You know…" His voice was hesitant like someone testing the water, poking their toe into a swimming pool. "What do you think about Michael? We kind of talked about it the other day, but not much."

I took a deep breath. I wanted to say that Michael was too much. I wanted to say that it drove me nuts how he was always giving little bits of parental advice. I hated his calendar of things for us to do and his organic food obsession. What finally came out was, "He rides a bike covered in glitter. With a unicorn head on it."

A smile twitched over dad's lips. "He does."

"It's so bright," I said, even though it wasn't exactly what bothered me about it.

Dad turned at me. "Has Michael ever talked to you about Sam?"

I shook my head, not understanding how this would relate to the Uni-cycle. I was frustrated that I hadn't actually said what I meant, how annoyed I get by Michael.

"It's a sad story," Dad said. He paused like he was waiting for the story to line itself up. "Sam was Michael's first boyfriend. Michael was still in the closet to just about everyone else. Sam was out and proud. One night at a bar, some guys asked if they were gay. Michael said no, but Sam said yes. The two of them had an argument about it. Michael went home. Sam never did."

I looked out over the water. "What happened?" I asked.

Dad took a deep breath and continued, "The best they know, Sam got beat pretty bad. Maybe it was those guys at the bar, maybe not. Either way, they didn't find him until the next morning. He didn't make it."

"Oh."

"You mentioned that crazy bike," Dad continued. "It was something Michael made for the first time he was in a Pride parade. He said he had to make a big statement. For Sam."

I tried to imagine Michael closeted, pretending that he was straight. And now he wore rainbows, highlighted his hair and rode unicorns.

"I'm not telling you this so you feel sorry for Michael, or accept him, or even like him." Dad's voice was steady, like the breeze coming over the water. "But I do want you to understand him just a little bit more."

"Thanks," I said. I meant it.

CHAPTER

I snuck out of the apartment, leaving Michael to wash more walls. I walked down the stairs and sat on the stoop in the morning sunlight. I looked down at the Potentilla Fruticosa and the two circles of earth that we had uncovered. I went back to the rocks and started clearing the next circle. Before long, Sage sat beside me, helping me.

"I can't wait until we can plant some flowers in here," she said. "I'm dying to see a little beauty around here." She looked guiltily at the Potentilla Fruticosa. "Not that you're not beautiful," she added to them, as if the bushes had feelings.

"I don't really know why we're doing this," I said. Back when I first got the idea for the garden, I had visions of working rich soil, and cultivating growth, not rummaging around in dry rocks in the heavy heat.

"What do you mean?"

I stopped, looking down at my sore, dirty fingers. "Mr. Keeler will probably just say that we picked the wrong kind of daylily or that it's stupid or something."

"He wouldn't say it was stupid," Sage said. "But he's Mr. Keeler, so he probably will say something grouchy."

I knew what she meant. He just wasn't the type of person who admitted to liking stuff.

Sage looked at the bushes again. "Where has Mr. Keeler been, anyway?"

I shrugged. "He's probably avoiding the heat like the rest of us should be doing."

"Even if he doesn't like the flowers we pick," she said, "It's the thought that counts, right?"

"Sure," I said. But I wanted him to like the flowers. I wanted him to see the daylilies blooming in an orange blaze again.

We cleared two more spots. There were only four left to go. It was slower without Michael, but I wanted space from him. I was still thinking about him and Sam and the Uni-cycle.

Later that day, though, when Michael invited me to go grocery shopping for Mr. Keeler again, I said yes. Since Mr. Keeler hadn't been out to water the bushes, I assumed he still wasn't up for walking to the corner store.

As we walked down the front steps we passed the garden. "You know," Michael said, "we could just hop on the 4. There's a garden center down Lyndale where we could pick up whatever you were going to plant."

"Daylilies," I said.

Michael pursed his lips. I could tell he was trying not to say anything, but sure enough, he couldn't hold it in. "Are you sure?" Michael said.

"Yes," I said.

"Ecologically, it might be beneficial to think about getting some native species."

I stared hard at Michael. "We're going to plant daylilies."

Michael sighed. "Well," he said, "you're the man in charge."

My phone rang. It was Mom calling to tell me her tomatoes were in bloom.

"I just had to call," she said. "They have these little yellow flowers on them. I thought you'd be proud. Heck, I'm proud. I feel like my little baby plants just learned to walk or something."

"That's great," I said, feeling worse about the fact that I hadn't finished the garden over here.

After I hung up, Michael and I walked in

silence until we reached Real Foods. Michael pulled things from the shelves, dropping them into his basket. It was much of the same stuff as before: soups, fresh fruit, prunes.

Nissy was at the checkout again. "Are you and Michael best friends yet?"

I looked over at Michael loading the groceries. "Not quite," I said.

Nissy laughed. She scanned the two boxes of prunes. "Well, at least you two will stay regular."

Michael rolled his eyes, but laughed a little as he snatched the prunes from her. "Thank you, Nissy." he said.

As we turned onto Stevens Ave, I asked Michael why he was doing all of this for Mr. Keeler.

Michael sighed as we opened the door to our building. "As we say, 'He's family.'"

"What do you mean?" I remembered what Sage said about Michael viewing Mr. Keeler as a father-figure, but I didn't think that's what

Michael meant. We walked up the stairs to Mr. Keeler's floor.

"One day," said Michael, "I am going to be an old queen barking out my own orders. And I hope someone will buy me groceries every now and then."

Michael rapped on Mr. Keeler's door. "Mr. Keeler, it's us. Groceries!"

There was no answer.

He knocked again.

He tried the door knob. It was unlocked. Michael poked his head into the room. "Hello? Mr. Keeler?"

Michael opened the door all the way and stepped into the apartment. I followed him.

Michael gasped. His body froze.

I followed the line of his eyes. Mr. Keeler was lying on the floor of the apartment, not moving.

Michael dropped his bag of groceries and ran over to him. "Please, please be breathing," he begged. I put down my bag of groceries to help him roll Mr. Keeler onto his back. His skin was still warm.

Michael watched Mr. Keeler's thin chest rise and fall as he took out his cellphone and dialed.

"Yes," he said. "This is an emergency. I'm with a man who has lost consciousness. He is still breathing…"

As Michael carried on the conversation, I looked at Mr. Keeler. I squatted next to him and put my hand on his forehead. I don't know why but I saw it on TV.

Michael kept rattling things into the phone. I sat staring at Mr. Keeler, his chest rising and falling. Time seemed to freeze.

Suddenly, paramedics stormed into the apartment, lifting him onto a stretcher, pulling him down the hall.

Michael began looking desperately around. "Wallet, wallet, wallet," he said. I got up to help him look. I found it in a bowl near the door. Michael opened it. "ID and insurance."

He looked up at me. "I'll call you," he said, hurrying after the paramedics.

I stood for several minutes in the empty apartment, trying to process what had just happened. Finally, I saw the groceries. I unloaded them into Mr. Keeler's fridge, folding the bags carefully.

I stepped out into the hall and closed his door tightly, wondering if I should have looked for his keys to lock it. I walked slowly up the stairs. I sat on the couch, staring at the park across the street. I held my phone in my hand.

Before long, I started getting text updates.

At the Hospital

Getting an IV

Gained consciousness

Michael came home a few hours later. His face looked serious.

"Mr. Keeler had a stroke," he said. "The doctors say his heart is a mess. They are trying to stabilize him, but it's not looking good."

I just nodded.

"He's just getting old, Jeremiah," Michael said. "And frankly, his health is a mess. Smoking two packs of unfiltered cigarettes a day hasn't done him any favors, either." He reached out a hand to my shoulder.

"Yeah," I said. I really had no idea what I was supposed to be feeling. I felt stunned, kind of frozen. It's not like I had known Mr. Keeler for a long time, so I hadn't earned the right to freak out about this had I?

I stood up and started to the door.

"Do you want to talk about it?" Michael called to me.

"No," I said. I walked down the stairs, down to the stoop. I sat on the concrete steps, looking at the Potentilla Fruticosa bushes in their dry, stone beds. I needed to do something, anything.

I stared at the rocky garden, remembering what Mr. Keeler had told me. It used to have daylilies. It looked like the whole bed was on fire in August when they bloomed. I pictured where the flowers could be filling the large, rocky gaps.

I knelt down on the rocks, clearing patches, pushing the rough stones to the side to try to find the rich dirt beneath. The pain in my fingers cleared my head.

"You should have told me you were working."

I jumped. Sage stood behind me, a popsicle in her hand. She was as pink and frizzy as ever.

"Mr. Keeler had a stroke," I said, my voice cracking.

"Oh," said Sage as though that explained why I was clawing at the rocks. She sat down on the steps. "My grandma had a stroke."

"Yeah?" I said. "What happened?"

Sage looked up towards the clouds. "There were complications. She didn't make it." She looked down at me, her voice consoling. "But I bet he will. That old man's a fighter."

"Yeah," I said. "He is."

I went and sat next to her.

"Wait here." Sage stood up and darted into her building. She returned a few moments later with another popsicle and handed it to me.

"Is he in the hospital now?" she asked.

I nodded. I made myself eat the popsicle.

"They say that he's a mess."

"That sounds like Mr. Keeler alright," said Sage.

We finished our popsicles.

I knelt down on the rocks and went back to work. Sage sat beside me. As the streetlights came on, we cleared large circles until the black plastic showed through. One by one until the last spot was open.

"All eight are finished," I said.

"Not finished," Sage said. "They're started."

CHAPTER

The next morning, I felt agitated. I tried to read, but I couldn't concentrate. I finally settled on staring at the bright colors of Saturday morning cartoons. Dad joined me after a while. Soon, Michael had to leave for his weekend shift.

After we ate lunch, Dad suggested we go visit

Mr. Keeler. We changed into church clothes. On the way down the stairs, Dad stopped at the second floor. He turned down the hall towards Mr. Keeler's apartment.

"Let's pick up a few things," he said. He walked up to the door and opened it boldly. I followed him inside. It felt weird to be in here without Mr. Keeler. I had done it yesterday as I put away the groceries, but now it felt like breaking and entering.

"What are we doing?" I asked.

Dad smiled. "Hospitals are always sterile. He probably needs some things from home." Dad looked around the apartment like an eagle. He swooped down to pick up a plant from the windowsill and a paperback novel with a bookmark half through it. He went over to the couch, gathering the old quilt in his arms.

I saw a picture in a gold frame on the coffee table. What looked like a much younger Mr. Keeler stood next to a man with long, blond hair. They were smiling. Mr. Keeler's face looked a lot different with the smile. He looked ready to tell a joke, ready to laugh.

"I think we should bring this, too." I said, picking up the photo.

Dad nodded and said we had enough now. We took the things down to his truck and drove to Riverside Hospital.

When we got to Mr. Keeler's room, a nurse let us in. Mr. Keeler was lying on a large bed that somehow made him look small. Tubes and wires came out of him. His breathing was shallow. His eyes turned to watch us come into the room, but his head didn't move.

"Hi, Mr. Keeler," Dad said, his voice sounding unusually loud in the heavy silence of the room. "How are you feeling?"

Mr. Keeler huffed. "How do you think I feel?" he asked.

I held up the quilt. "We brought you a few things," I said. Dad helped me lay the blanket over his legs.

"What did you do? Break into my

apartment?" Mr. Keeler asked.

Dad smiled. "We sure did."

Dad put the plant on the windowsill and held out the book to Mr. Keeler, who half raised an arm, pointing to the tray next to him. Dad set it down.

I set the photo on Mr. Keeler's bedside table.

Mr. Keeler turned his eyes to stare at it for a long time.

"Need us to call anyone?" Dad asked. "Family or friends or anyone?"

Mr. Keeler let out a laugh that sounded like a cough. "I don't have anyone left. I outlasted everyone else."

"We're here," Dad said.

Mr. Keeler looked up at the ceiling. "My sister is flying up from Albuquerque."

"Good," Dad said.

"She's a witch." Mr. Keeler laid back and closed his eyes.

We sat for a while in silence before Dad picked up the book and began to read out loud. It was a Stephen King novel. The bookmark opened to a particularly grisly chapter, but Dad plowed forward, occasionally wincing, looking at me apologetically.

The nurse came in. "What are you gentlemen talking about in here?"

Dad held up the book, his face turning slightly pink.

"Mr. Keeler," the nurse said past us, "I think you're going to have to end your bedtime story there." She turned back to us. "Visiting hours are over."

We had spent the entire afternoon.

"Bye," I said.

Dad saluted. "Pleasant dreams, Sir," he said.

Mr. Keeler snorted. "Yeah," he said.

We drove home in silence. After Dad parked the truck, we walked up to our building. Dark patches of plastic still showed through the places Sage and I had scratched free of rocks.

"Dad," I said. "We need to plant the garden."

Dad nodded, his eyebrows going up. "Well,"

he said, "I know just the place to pick up a few plants."

We drove down Lyndale, probably to the same place Michael was talking about.

When we walked into the greenhouse, I recognized the employee at once. It was Robi, Dad and Michael's friend from Cocktail Hour.

Robi smiled and walked over to us. "How can I help you gentlemen?" Robi asked.

Dad turned to me. "Do you know what you want?"

"Yes," I said. "I know exactly what I want."

I picked out eight large daylilies. The tags showed they would be a fiery orange when they bloomed. Several of them had buds stretching up above their grassy leaves.

Robi made sure we didn't leave without two bags of manure to work into the soil.

Dad made us stop for tacos on the way back to our apartment. I hadn't realized I was so hungry.

By the time we came back to our building, the

streetlights had come on.

Dad pulled a shovel from the back of his truck. We dug the hard earth, breaking up the pieces. We removed some of the old soil, replacing it with the rich manure, working it together.

Mosquitos came out. The moon rose over downtown. When all eight holes were dug, we removed the first daylily from its plastic pot.

"These plants get root-bound," I said, pointing to the tangled mass of white roots that still kept the shape of the pot. "I read that you have to break the roots to stimulate new growth. If you don't break them up, they won't stretch out into the earth around them."

Even though I knew I needed to, it felt wrong to break apart the roots which clung so tightly to the soil they had known for so long.

As we patted the dirt around the fourth plant, Michael came riding up on the Uni-cycle. He leaned it against the stoop and came over to help even though he was still in his work uniform.

He didn't say anything about the plants being an invasive species.

"This garden was supposed to be for Mr. Keeler," I said.

"I know," Michael said. "Let's hope he can get back here to see it."

Together, we finished planting. Dad went upstairs and brought down a large pitcher. One by one, we watered in the plants. Then I watered each of Mr. Keeler's Potentilla Fruticosa which didn't look quite so alone anymore. I looked at the lily buds stretching up towards the sky. They would bloom soon.

"They'll be perfect," Michael said. "They were the right selection, Jeremiah."

CHAPTER

(16)

It was a windy morning. On the way back from church, Dad said a new weather system was blowing through. Life should be a little easier. Or at least cooler.

I sat in front on the stoop as Dad and Michael went upstairs, talking about the morning sermon.

Soon enough, Sage came out. She called a hello, but then her face fell.

"You planted the garden," she said.

"Yeah," I said, feeling a smile break across my face. "Last night. Dad and me. And Michael."

"I thought," her voice sounded hurt, "I thought we were going to plant the garden."

I looked at her, not quite sure what to do or say. Really? She was upset that the garden was planted?

"I helped clear rocks," she said. "I sat out in the horrible heat and dug through the rocks and scraped up my fingers." She held up her hand as proof.

I was annoyed. Maybe it was just the stress of the last couple of days. Maybe it was something else. I felt like if anyone had a right to be upset, it was me. I had a friend in the hospital.

"So what?" I said. "Are you really going to cry about it?"

Sage stared hard at me, then turned, storming toward her building. "Maybe," she yelled.

"Maybe I am."

I sat for a long time until my breathing leveled out. Then I went upstairs for a pitcher. I brought it down and watered the plants.

I didn't see Sage Monday morning. I wondered if she was still mad about the garden. Maybe she was avoiding me. Part of me wanted to walk up to her building and buzz her apartment, but the stubborn part won out and I didn't.

That afternoon, Michael and I visited Mr. Keeler. He had been transferred to a new room. I noticed that all of the things Dad and I brought for him had been transferred as well. The picture now sat on Mr. Keeler's tray next to his bed.

The nurse said he was still experiencing some complications. He would have to stay until they got everything sorted out.

We sat with him. Michael tried to make small talk, which Mr. Keeler continually shot down.

I thought about telling him we had planted the daylilies, but I held off. It would be a better surprise for him to come home to them already planted, hopefully blooming.

Finally, we said our goodbyes and headed home.

On the bus back to the apartment, I told Michael about what happened with Sage and her outburst over the planted garden.

"You know, you could go over there and tell her you're sorry," Michael said.

"Why?" I said. "I didn't do anything wrong."

"Well," Michael said. "You can waste a lot of time being stubborn."

It was true. I could.

The next morning, I walked down the stairs out of habit, not thinking about the fact that Sage and I were fighting. Weren't we? But there she was, walking through the garden, touching each of the buds, which were turning fat and orange.

She looked up at me. "Sorry," she said before I could say anything.

I swallowed my pride. "I'm sorry, too. I just got kind of caught up. I wanted the garden to be complete for Mr. Keeler."

"Is he going to die?" Sage asked it so directly I just stared at her for a minute.

"I don't know. Maybe."

Sage looked out over the garden. "You did the right thing. I was just so bummed. There were flowers at my old house, but I never got to plant any."

I suddenly felt sorry for Sage, not being able to be a part of planting. "I have an idea." I said. "What if we went and got a few annuals? The daylilies will spread and fill the gaps next year, but this year, they need some company."

It was true. I know the plants needed us to dig up those big circles, but the wide band of earth around each plant looked as empty and sad as the rocks.

Sage's eyes lit up. "We could do that?"

"Sure," I said. "I think you should pick them out."

We went upstairs to tell Michael that we needed to go back out to the greenhouse.

"I could come along," he offered. "I have a basket on the Uni-cycle so we could bring the plants home."

I hadn't thought about that. We could do it on our bicycles. But I still didn't want to be seen with the Uni-cycle.

We decided to take the bus, and Michael insisted on joining us. He said he didn't mind us riding around the neighborhood, but he thought adult supervision was necessary when it came to public transit. Whatever.

Once Sage got the okay from Reina, we took the 4 down Lyndale. Robi was working again.

When Sage met Robi, she stared for a moment, then asked, "What pronouns do you use?"

Robi looked impressed. "I appreciate you asking. I prefer they, theirs, them."

Sage nodded. "Robi," she said, "We need flowers. The pinkest flowers you have."

Why had I promised Sage she could pick the flowers? She chose a tray of magenta petunias. Of course.

On the way back, Sage smiled down at her plants. "I like Robi. They understood exactly what I needed."

"How did you know to ask about pronouns?" I asked Sage.

"Robi looked like they might like other pronouns," Sage said. "But you can't really tell by looking. I always try to ask whenever I remember. Speaking of which, what pronouns do you use?"

"He and him, I guess," I said. I had never really thought about it.

"I try to ask, too," Michael said. "There is a large spectrum of gender expression and a deep pool of pronouns to choose from."

"A pool," Sage said. "I like that. A pool of pronouns. Like you could dive in and swim around until you found the right ones, *your* pronouns."

"Which ones would you pick?" I asked.

She considered. "Well, maybe *she* and *her*, but I would find the ones that bobbed up to the surface no matter how many times you dunked them. Or maybe a giant inflated HERS you could bat back and forth like a beach ball." She turned to me. "I'm guessing you would probably dig your pronouns out of the ground," she said to me. "Not find them in a pool."

"And you," I said to Michael, "would find them in the produce section of Real Foods."

"Please," Michael said. "I gathered my *he, him, his* from the glittering dust of a unicorn."

Sage squealed, and even I couldn't help laughing.

When we got back to our building, we planted a perimeter of petunias in the soft earth around each daylily, keeping them as close to the stones as possible. Reina came out to help. With Reina, Michael, Sage and me all working, it wasn't long before the pink flowers were in.

As we used pitchers to water the flowers, Sage was practically glowing. "Now this is a garden. It's just not happy without pink."

"Indeed," Michael smiled. I realized I was smiling, too.

CHAPTER

Michael started painting the bathroom. The song "Ain't No Mountain High Enough" echoed in the small room.

When the first coat of paint was done, I asked if we could visit Mr. Keeler again. Michael changed out of his painting clothes.

As we walked down to the bus, he told me we

could paint my room next.

"You can pick any color you want," he said. "Except peach. And you'll have to help me."

"Okay." As we boarded the bus to the hospital, I was surprised at myself. It no longer sounded like a horrible thing to work on a project with Michael. When had *that* changed?

When we got to Mr. Keeler's room, the back of his bed was raised so he was in a half-upright position, his old quilt draped over his legs.

"You look chipper," Michael said.

Mr. Keeler grunted.

"Are you comfortable?" Michael asked.

Mr. Keeler huffed. "Do I look comfortable?"

"You let us know if you need anything," Michael said, his voice firmly even.

Mr. Keeler wheezed. "The thing I could really use is a cigarette."

Michael sighed, then stood up. He stepped out of the room. Through the glass, I could see him beckoning to a nurse. They leaned towards each other to talk too quietly for us to hear.

"I can hear you," Mr. Keeler half rose as he called to them. Then he fell back into bed. "They think I'll die. But I'll fight. Life is a fight." He took several long, wheezing breaths, then looked at me, "Remember that."

I sat by his bed. He lay back, his eyes half open.

Michael came back into the room. "Will you be okay here for a few minutes?" he asked me.

I shrugged. "Sure."

He left. I looked back at Mr. Keeler. I didn't know what to say to him. I looked around the room, then settled on the picture.

"Mr. Keeler?" I asked. He opened his eyes. I took a deep breath. "Who's in that picture?"

Mr. Keeler's eyes rested on the gold frame. "Charlie," he said. "He was my partner."

"Is he..." I hesitated. "Did he—"

"Die?" Mr. Keeler cut in. "April 8, 2007."

"I'm sorry." I said.

"We were the last ones," he said. "Our building," he paused to take several breaths.

Finally, Mr. Keeler went on. "It was full of us. So many died in the '80s. AIDS. But Charlie and I. We survived. We stayed."

He looked at me. "Now it's all gone." He began to cough.

I watched him regain his breath. I hesitated, then decided to just go ahead and tell him. It felt like he needed to hear something good.

"We made a garden in front of our building," I said. "It has daylilies. Just like it used to." I decided to leave out Sage's magenta petunias.

"And the Potentilla Fruticosa?" Mr. Keeler's eyes narrowed at me.

"They're there. But they're not so alone now. It's not super impressive, but everything will grow. There will be more next year."

"Don't forget to water it," he said. I thought I saw the faintest hint of a smile on his face. He lay back, breathing heavily.

"You'll see it soon," I told him, although I was beginning to fear he wouldn't.

We sat in silence until Michael returned, his

face slightly pink. He held out a package of cigarettes. Mr. Keeler lifted a shaky hand to receive them.

"Filters?" he said. "We're past the need for filters."

Michael rolled his eyes. "Mr. Keeler—"

"Get me outside," Mr. Keeler interrupted. "I need one."

The nurse helped us move Mr. Keeler into a wheelchair. His IV hung above him like his own personal rain cloud. I wondered what Sage would name it. We took the elevator down several floors until we could wheel outside into the late July sunshine.

Mr. Keeler fumbled for a while, trying to open the pack. Michael held out his hand, but Mr. Keeler handed the cigarettes to me. I peeled off the shiny wrapper. I had never held a pack of cigarettes before. My fingers felt nervous being watched by both of them, but I fished one out of the foil liner easily enough.

Michael lit the cigarette and handed it to Mr.

Keeler. Mr. Keeler's hands were shaking too much to hold it. It fell to the ground. Michael carefully put it out and tossed it into a bucket of sand with a bunch of cigarette butts.

The same thing happened to the next cigarette.

Michael stood over Mr. Keeler and sighed. Then he squatted next to Mr. Keeler, took another cigarette, lit it, and held it out to Mr. Keeler's mouth.

I expected Mr. Keeler to turn away. Instead, he leaned in, curled his lips around the end of the cigarette, and breathed deep. His eyes closed, his head tilted back, he smiled. He opened his mouth, letting the smoke escape over his face.

"Stay over there, Jeremiah," Michael commanded. "I don't want you getting any of this second-hand smoke."

It was weird watching the two of them, enemies, connected by a cigarette, something Michael hated about Mr. Keeler. Each draw on the cigarette, they moved close for an instant, connected, then pulled back.

When Mr. Keeler had exhausted the cigarette, Michael ground the tip on the sidewalk. He held it for a moment, Mr. Keeler watching through the slits of his eyes. Michael rolled the butt of the cigarette between his fingers, then flicked it onto the sidewalk, an almost perfect impression of Mr. Keeler.

"Not bad," Mr. Keeler wheezed. "You'll be a man yet."

Michael stood up behind the chair and took a deep breath, shaking his head.

"Here," Michael said, handing over the chair to me. "You can wheel this crabby old thing."

I took the handles to the wheelchair. As I began to push Mr. Keeler back towards the building, I noticed Michael stoop down, pick up the cigarette butt and place it in the bucket with the others.

Back upstairs, the nurse helped us move Mr. Keeler back into his bed.

"Don't wait so long next time," Mr. Keeler said as we readied ourselves to go. "I'll need another smoke."

"Okay," I said, following Michael towards the hallway.

"Get out already," Mr. Keeler nodded toward the door. He smiled a tiny smile at me, then lay back and closed his eyes. "Wait. Don't come tomorrow," he said. "My sister's coming."

I laughed. "Okay."

On the bus ride back, Michael was quiet. We watched shops and businesses roll past our window.

"You know, Jeremiah," Michael said. "They say he's not looking good."

I kept staring out the window.

Michael went on. "His health is a mess."

"Is he going to die?"

"We don't know, Jeremiah," Michael said. "But we can hope he has enough fight in him."

CHAPTER

Sage and I circled the neighborhood
on our bikes, going nowhere in particular. We
ended at the Mia, the Minneapolis Institute of
the Arts, wandering among the paintings.

We stopped in front of *The Studio* again.

"When we planted the garden," Sage said. "I
felt like that." She pointed to the picture. "I felt

like this." She stood with her hands over her head, victorious.

I smiled. "I think I'll feel like that when Mr. Keeler sees the garden," I said. I hoped that everything was okay with his sister. Then again, for all I knew, he could be best friends with her. It was hard to tell with Mr. Keeler.

I hoped he would see it. I really hoped.

When we walked out the doors and down the steps of the building, the sky was clear and blue.

Sage frowned up at the bright sky. "Sunlight. Sometimes I feel like the clouds are hiding from me."

I decided to ask her something I had been wondering. "Do you ever wish that you were part of a..." I searched for the right word. "I don't know...a normal family?"

To my surprise, Sage laughed. "I don't even know what that means," she said, looking away from the sky to me. "When I was a little kid, I thought I was in the most normal family in the world. It wasn't until school that I started to see how weird my family is. How weird every family is."

"I guess," I said. I hesitated, then spoke slowly, softly. "Sometimes, I wish I was in a normal family."

"Really?" Sage said, "No offense, but your parents are divorced. That's about as normal as you can get."

There was something about the way she said it, something about the sparkle in her face that made me start laughing. She laughed, too.

"Okay," I finally said.

We walked back. We stopped in front of the garden.

"I wish he would come home already," Sage said. "I'm in agony waiting for him to return so we can show him this. Look," Sage said, her hand pointing at one of the daylilies. The orange bud had burst into bloom, the first one. The flower was a bright, fiery orange. "It's a sign," Sage said.

I got an idea. I pulled out my pocket knife.

"Michael and I are visiting today. We could bring a little garden to him."

"Careful," Sage said. "That's what got me in trouble with him the first time we met."

"Desperate times call for desperate measures," I said.

The other daylilies had several buds, but weren't blooming yet. I carefully cut through several woody branches of the Potentilla Fruticosa and the soft stems of the loud petunias. Sage arranged them. Then I cut the stem beneath the daylily. Sage stuck it into the center of her bouquet. The orange, magenta, and gold were intense in the sunlight.

We took our bouquet upstairs and rummaged around in the kitchen for a vase.

Michael found us. "For Mr. Keeler?" he asked. I nodded.

Michael sighed, but he was smiling. "Well. Let's go."

I turned to Sage. "Do you want to come, too?"

Sage nodded slowly. "Yes. I do."

All together, we travelled to the bus stop, Sage carefully carrying the vase of flowers. The sun was bright and warm, making the city glow. We arrived at the hospital, and went up the elevator to Mr. Keeler's room.

When we arrived at his room, it was empty. We stood for a moment, staring at the open space.

"He must have changed rooms," Michael said. We followed him to the nurses' station.

"We're here to see Gregory Keeler," he said. "He was in room 412."

The nurse nodded. "I have some bad news," she said. "Would you like to sit down?"

"No," I said, my stomach getting heavy. "Just tell us."

"I'm afraid Mr. Keeler experienced more complications last night. It was sudden." She looked at each of our faces in turn. "We did what we could. I'm so sorry, he passed away."

We stood for a moment, frozen.

"His sister arrived in time to say goodbye," the nurse said. "She's taking care of the details."

"Is she here?" Michael asked, looking around as if Mr. Keeler's sister was about to step out of a doorway to talk to us.

"I don't know where she is," the nurse said. "She was here late into the night. She probably needs to get some rest."

"So," Michael finally said. "Should we do anything? Like is there anything that needs to be done now? I mean, we're just his neighbors, but…"

The nurse shook her head. "His sister is taking care of the details."

We stood, not moving.

"I'm sorry," the nurse said again.

"Yeah," Michael said. "Thank you."

We stood in a silent circle for a few more moments before Michael broke us out of the silence, pulling us towards the elevators.

"Shoot," he said. "Shoot. Shoot, shoot, shoot."

As the elevator descended, he put a hand on each of our shoulders. "Sorry, guys. I'm so sorry."

We followed Michael out of the hospital. The sun was bright, unmercifully shining down, casting the city into a sticky haze.

I looked over at Sage. Her eyes were large, stunned. She held the flowers uselessly in her hand.

Michael led us back towards the bus stop in silence. As we waited for the bus, Sage took a shuddering breath.

She stood up. "What about these?" she said, holding the flowers. Her voice was loud. "Shouldn't they go to his body or something?"

Michael looked down at her. "It's too late. It's out of our hands."

Sage narrowed her eyes. "Well, they're still in my hands." She stormed out of the bus stop. Michael ran after her. I followed behind.

She stopped. "This isn't how it's supposed to work." Her voice sounded more angry than sad. "People aren't just supposed to die and disappear. When is his funeral? When's his wake? His memorial?"

"His sister will probably take his body or ashes down to Albuquerque," Michael said with a sigh.

I stood next to Sage. "So that's it?" I asked, my voice breaking. "That's all?" I fought to keep my voice level.

Michael knelt down beside us. To my surprise, there were actual tears in his eyes.

"Yeah," he said. "It's done. That's all. I wish it wasn't."

Michael took a deep breath. Sage and I followed him back to the bus stop. We rode home in silence.

CHAPTER

When we got back to Stevens Square from the hospital, the three of us stood, staring at the garden.

"Are you okay?" Michael asked, putting a hand on my shoulder.

I shrugged. I swallowed, hoping to steady my voice. "I didn't know him that well," I said, trying not to sound like I was about to cry.

Sage reached out a hand and took mine.

The three of us stood side by side, staring at the garden. I remembered watching Mr. Keeler walking over the rocks, the watering can held tight.

Now there was a garden. The daylilies were ready to burst into meaningless bloom.

All afternoon Michael kept trying to talk about it, pressing me to talk too. But I didn't want to. I didn't know how I was supposed to feel. I had barely known Mr. Keeler, but it felt like he had become part of my life.

When Dad and I went for a ride that night, he asked if I wanted to talk about Mr. Keeler, too, but I said no. Dad didn't push the matter.

It's funny how, when someone leaves, the earth doesn't seem to notice. The next several days, life went on as normal. Really, what part did Mr. Keeler have in my life except to bring down the watering can and make fun of Michael?

Saturday night, we went to a Twins game, sitting in a section reserved for the Pride group. The people around me cheered. I tried to watch the game. Sunday, we went to church. I watered the garden. We went out for Vietnamese food.

Life seemed like it had already moved on. But I hadn't.

Then, on Monday afternoon, a woman came to our building while Sage and I were watering the garden. She introduced herself as Mrs. Tofte, Mr. Keeler's sister. She had the same nose and fierce eyes, but they were softened by her smiles. We took her inside to Maxine's office.

Maxine led Mrs. Tofte upstairs, carrying several papers.

Soon, Michael, Sage, and I were helping her go through his things, piling them into black garbage bags to take to Salvation Army, his whole life stuffed in like trash.

Mrs. Tofte had a file box where she put "significant items" to take home. A bowl of jewelry from his desk. His glasses from his night stand. His lighter.

She said they had cremated the body.

She said there would be a service in Albuquerque.

She said we were sweet to help her.

Michael said he could take the food items to the local food bank and packed up all the soup and nonperishable food we had brought Mr. Keeler.

When I handed Mrs. Tofte the watering can to put with the significant items, she gestured towards the donation bags.

I hesitated, then asked if I could keep it.

She smiled at me, her eyes sad and tired. "Yes," she said. "Of course."

A truck came, and two men took away all of the furniture and the bags. The apartment was empty except for a few things here and there that would be dealt with by the cleaning people. Even with everything gone, there was still the faint smell of cigarette smoke, hanging like a memory.

"He loved this place," Mrs. Tofte told us. "He and Charlie. They were so happy here."

Michael carried the box down the steps to Mrs. Tofte's car. Mrs. Tofte thanked us, waved, and then she was gone.

He was gone.

The rest of the week felt empty. I used the old watering can to keep the plants thriving under the bright sun.

We prepped my room and applied the first coat of Cool Shale to the walls.

I got through several more chapters of *The Grapes of Wrath*.

Thursday morning, Sage and I were lying on the grass in the park again.

"This is weird," Sage said. "Mr. Keeler's spirit isn't going to move on from here until we let him go. I thought I just saw him over there watering."

"I have an idea," she said. "Get your bike."

I met her in the back alley with my bike. She was carrying the same bouquet we had made for

Mr. Keeler the day he died. It was wilted and browning. I had forgotten about it.

"Follow me," she said.

We rode through downtown all the way to the Mississippi River. The water sparkled in the morning light. I could see the Stone Arch Bridge just downstream. We locked our bikes and walked to a railing. The river flowed steady before us.

"Mr. Keeler," Sage said. "We miss you. I thought you were scary until I knew you liked flowers. I wish you could have seen the garden. It's beautiful. Every day new daylilies open."

She looked at me expectantly. I knew how this type of thing was supposed to work. I had read this scenario a million times in books. Everyone would say something poetic or meaningful. But standing here now it was hard to say anything.

I took a deep breath. "Honestly," I said, "I liked how he, or you, I guess—" I looked at the shimmering water. "I liked how stubborn you were. I liked that you didn't give an inch. And I liked how you always left it to Michael pick up your cigarette butts."

As I said this, I suddenly realized how one of the things I had liked so much about Mr. Keeler was that he was able to antagonize Michael.

Michael, who had bought him groceries. Michael, who had helped pick away the rocks and plant the daylilies. Michael, who had even helped him smoke that last cigarette. Michael, who I had been so sure I didn't like. I wasn't so sure anymore.

I looked back at the withered bouquet. "Goodbye," I said.

Sage shook her head. "See you later," she corrected.

She threw the bouquet. The wind caught it. Instead of falling to the moving Mississippi below, it landed on one of the concrete footings.

We stared at it. The crinkled leaves waved slightly in the breeze.

Suddenly Sage laughed.

"So much for that moment," she said.

I looked down and smiled. Maybe that was more accurate. Things don't just wash down the river. Sometimes the things you want to throw far away from you keep sitting there in front of you while you have to keep on living. We watched the water move past the bouquet for a long time.

Finally, Sage and I sat down on a bench. The clouds moved over our heads, oblivious to the stuff we faced here below. We watched them float past.

"That one," I said pointing to a large cloud nearing the sun. "That one is Mr. Keeler if I've ever seen him."

"It is." I could hear the smile in Sage's voice.

The cloud finally covered the sun, the edges of it turning golden.

"See?" Sage said. "It tries to hide the light, but it just becomes luminescent."

We watched as the cloud glowed, then shifted, releasing the rays of the sun, making room for the next one.

CHAPTER

(20)

As Michael helped me roll the final coat
of paint onto my walls, his phone rang. Michael
set down his roller, hitting speaker phone. It was
Dad.

"Heather and Dave are in labor," Dad said.

"Is everything alright?" Michael asked, all of a
sudden tense.

"Yes," Dad said. "But they were supposed to host Cocktail Hour tonight."

"And let me guess," Michael interrupted. "You invited everyone over here." Michael looked over at me as he said this. I smiled and rolled my eyes with him. With him, not at him. Since when did I do that?

"No, actually," Dad said. "I was about to, but I remembered what you said. I'm calling to run it past you first."

"Oh," Michael said. "Oh. Yeah. Okay. That would actually be fine."

"Thanks, Love," Dad said.

They hung up.

Michael looked at me, his eyebrows raised. "Your father will never cease to amaze me."

"For real," I said.

When Dad got home, Michael stopped him in the doorway.

"Thank you," he said. "Really, that meant a lot." He pulled Dad into a big kiss. I blushed and looked away, but realized I was smiling a little.

After supper when everyone arrived, Michael invited me to stay. I looked out the window. Sage sat in the park waiting for me.

"Just a minute," I said.

I pulled Sage upstairs to the apartment. I introduced her. Nobody made jokes about whether or not we were boyfriend and girlfriend. We sat next to Mary and Jo. Michael handed us two iced teas with lemon.

Sage and I sat and listened as the conversation moved along. It was my first time, so I just sipped my drink while everyone else talked. Emily made plans for meal deliveries to Heather and Dave while they "acclimate to the raging storm of parenthood."

Then the conversation roamed from the upcoming election to the farmer's market on Saturday, to marriage equality.

"I know it's legal," Big Ben said. "But I can't see myself ever marrying."

"Why?" Robi asked. "You and Jon have been

together forever."

"21 years this April," Jon said, his face glowing.

"Marriage is so heteronormative," Ben said. "Isn't the best part of being gay the ability to shun all of that?"

"I don't know," Michael said. "I would like to get married. And not just for tax reasons."

Everyone laughed.

Dad and Michael exchanged a look. I watched as they shared a brief quiet moment. They wanted to get married. I had expected this. Feared this. But as I watched the look pass between Dad and Michael, I realized something had changed inside me.

They wanted to marry. And I didn't think I hated the idea anymore.

The next day, Friday, Michael picked up his cell phone during supper to open a text. His face lit up. "Heather and Dave," he said. "After a grueling labor, Gordon William Richards was born last night. Seven pounds, 10 ounces."

The phone beeped again, and Michael held out a picture of a squashed, pink face in a little red hat. It reminded me of the garden gnome in my grandma's front yard. "Adorable," I said.

A smile broke out over Dad's face. "Looks like a little prize fighter."

"I want one," Michael said, looking like he was about to melt.

"It's a baby, not a Pokémon card," I said.

"Which hospital?" Dad asked.

"Riverside," Michael said. It was the same hospital where Mr. Keeler had died.

"Another life hits the earth," Dad said.

Later, after Michael went to work, Dad and I went downstairs to get our bikes.

"We've got plenty of time before dark," Dad said as we came out the back into the alley. "Greenway?"

I nodded.

I followed him, even though I knew how to get to the Greenway by now.

Moving through the air made it feel cooler

even though sweat still rolled down my face. Dad was a little slower tonight, more relaxed.

We merged onto the Greenway and rode through the growing shadows.

When we passed the Girard Street ramp, I thought again about Michael and Dad meeting there almost a year ago. It was such an ordinary place. Maybe that's where most magical things happen.

"Let's stop at Lake Bde Maka Ska again," I said. Dad nodded.

When we came to the lake, Dad and I locked our bikes at our usual beach. The sun turned the waves into diamonds. We sat on the warm sand.

Dad skipped a rock. "The summer's almost done," he said. "August is just about here."

I opened my mouth, then bit my lip. I watched two little kids splashing in the water.

"Are you going to marry Michael?" I finally asked.

Dad smiled at me, then looked out at the water. The wind blew his hair wildly around his head. "I would like to," he said, then stopped.

"But?" I asked.

Dad looked out at the water, then stared at me for a long time. "Michael isn't quite ready. He..." Dad took a deep breath. "He said he wants to wait until he knows whether you approve."

"You're waiting for me?" I was surprised.

"Yes and no," Dad said. "Believe me, Jeremiah, your opinion means a whole lot to me, but I've lived too much of my life waiting for other people's approval. To me, if I think I should marry Michael, I'm going to do it."

I nodded.

"But," he continued, "your opinion means a whole lot."

"You have my approval," I said. "Whether or not it matters."

"You mean it?" Dad asked testing, "I thought you didn't like Michael."

"I thought so, too," I said. "I think I was wrong."

Dad was quiet for a long time, sitting perfectly still. From the look in his eyes, I could tell that his brain was working. "I do have a plan for the proposal," Dad said. "And I was wondering if you would be a part of it. You could show Michael you approve."

"Sure," I said, a smile opening across my face. "What's the plan?"

Unlike most plans that Dad created, this one required waiting for over a week.

CHAPTER

"They're getting engaged," I told Mom on the phone. I was surprised at the excitement I heard in my own voice. "They're getting engaged next Saturday."

"Wait," Mom said. "Your father has actually made a plan for the future? That's a first."

"What about your engagement?" I asked.

Mom laughed. "Totally off the cuff. He didn't even have a ring. So, what's Al's plan?"

"It's going to be at the place they first met," I said. "I'm going to deliver the ring. Dad said it's really important to Michael to know I approve."

I hesitated, then asked the question I had been wondering. "Are you okay with all this? Does it bother you?"

"Why would it bother me?" Mom asked.

"I don't know," I said. I was worried about telling her what I actually thought. "I've just noticed that you never tried to find someone else. It almost feels like you're waiting. For him."

Mom sighed. "I could not be happier for Al. I've served my time with him, but I don't want to go back. We broke up because we were incompatible. That hasn't changed."

I took a deep breath. "It wasn't because he's..." I hesitated. "Because he's interested in men?"

"He's bisexual," Mom said. "Trust me; he was

very interested in me back in the day."

I took a deep breath, but couldn't think of what to say.

"Do you think that's why we broke up?" Mom sounded surprised. "I don't care that he's bi. I knew that going into the relationship. We broke up because we are two peas in a pod. That's what was so fun at first. Everything we did was spontaneous, off the wall. But we were stuck. We were driving each other crazy. We separated and then divorced. Your dad needed to find someone to stabilize him."

I thought about Michael and the stability he brought to Dad, making meals, planning ahead, actually using a calendar.

Mom kept talking. "I could not be happier for Al. And Michael. And you. Who knew you would be getting a second dad this summer?"

"Not me," I said. Before I hung up, I asked how her tomatoes were doing.

"They are thriving," Mom said. "I can't wait till you get home. They should keep producing until it frosts. You'll get to see them."

The next week flew by. We went and visited Dave and Heather and tiny Gordon. Michael had that melty expression as he held the baby. Dad's face lit up when he took a turn holding the newborn. I felt a surprising stab of jealousy even though I knew it was stupid.

That week, back at the apartment, Michael and I finished painting the hallway, the very last room of the apartment. It went quickly, taking barely any time to finish the small space.

I finalized plans with Sage for the big day. She was going to join me in my ring delivery since Dad still didn't want me to ride through the city by myself.

We took several rides to the Girard Street exit, timing our rides so we could know just when to begin our ride Saturday morning.

Finally, it was Friday, the night before the art festival. The night before the engagement. The night before Sage and I would ride our bikes out to the Girard Street exit and give Dad and

Michael the ring.

"You still on?" Dad asked in a whisper.

I nodded.

"Don't be late," Dad said, winking at me.

"I won't."

The next morning, I woke up early. This wasn't part of the plan, but I was excited. Everything was ready.

I tried to read another chapter of *Grapes of Wrath*, but I couldn't concentrate. I walked to the living room and slouched on the couch, watching TV.

Dad woke up next. He sat next to me. Although he didn't say anything, he was smiling to himself.

"How are you feeling?" I asked in a low voice.

Dad's face turned a little pink. He scratched behind his ear. "I'm excited."

Soon we heard Michael go into the bathroom and the shower turn on. Finally, Michael walked out, his hair perfectly styled, wearing paisley print shorts.

"Let's bounce," Michael said.

Dad got up.

I stayed on the couch. "I'm not up for it."

"No!" Michael said it like there was no possible way that I could not go to the art festival. "What's wrong? You can't miss the festival. This has been on our calendar for months."

I shrugged. "You guys go ahead. I'll hang out here."

Dad stepped in before Michael got carried away. "He doesn't have to. You sure, Jeremiah?"

"Yeah," I said. I was trying to act nonchalant, like I wasn't jittery and nervous. "I just don't feel like going."

"You have no idea what you're missing out on," Michael said. "It's nearly criminal."

"I'm not up for it today," I said.

Michael kept pestering me. "We're taking the bus. You won't have to exert yourself to get there."

Dad moved towards the door and pulled on

his bi flag hat. "He's fine. We'll see you later, Jeremiah." Dad pushed Michael out the door and poked his head in to give me a big wink.

I waited until their footsteps faded down the back steps. I went to my room and put on a clean button-up shirt. I checked myself in the mirror, combing my shaggy hair. I don't know why; I wasn't the one getting engaged today.

I reached behind my books to where I had hidden the ring box. I opened it to make sure the band hadn't disappeared during the night. The band was wide, dotted with five small diamonds nestled into the gold. I shut the box and placed it into one of the zippered pockets of my cargo shorts, then grabbed my bike helmet.

When I went out the front door, Sage was already waiting for me on the front stoop, her face shining.

"The lilies." She pointed to the garden. The daylilies were blooming, bright and fiery in the morning light. It felt like a good omen. I hoped that Mr. Keeler could see it somehow.

Sage and I stared for a few moments at the lilies, then walked across the street to the park.

Now came the hard part. Waiting. Dad wanted time to get Michael to the festival and wander around for a few minutes before pulling him away down the ramp where they first met, and he would "recall a few memories" before we rode up at 11:00. It was only a 16-minute ride. The plan was to hang out in the park until 10:35, then get our bikes, leaving us plenty of time to ride out.

Sage and I walked across the street to the park. We sat in the shade.

"Maybe we should just go." Sage said. "I hate waiting."

I shook my head. "It's all part of the plan. It would be weird if we were just sitting there at the bottom of the ramp when Dad and Michael started to walk down it."

"Agony." Sage lay back, looking up at the sky through the waving leaves.

Sage kept a close watch on the time. People

walked past with their dogs. A mother came with her toddler to play on the small playground. Finally, Sage looked at her watch.

"10:35." Her voice was high with excitement.

"See you in a minute." We parted to our separate buildings. I brought my bicycle up to the alley behind our building. Sage was there, straddling her bike, her helmet already clipped.

"Ready?" she asked.

I put on my own helmet and swung my leg over the crossbar. My feet were ready for the ride.

I took a deep breath. "Yes." I said.

"The ring?"

I patted my pocket.

It was still a little weird to me that Sage would be joining me for one of the bigger moments of my life so far, but with Sage, it just felt right somehow.

"10:39," Sage called as we began cycling down the alley. Everything was going according to plan. We should have plenty enough time to ride down to the Greenway and pedal to the Girard Street exit.

Dad and Michael would be there. Dad would probably be standing there telling Michael all sorts of memories from their year together.

We began to pick up speed in the alley. I looked up to tell Sage to watch out for potholes. It would be a joke. Michael always had to say it in his parental voice when we were biking this way.

The words never came out of my mouth.

It happened fast!

My bike jerked. My body jarred. I flew forward into my handlebars. I heard what I thought was a gunshot.

It was my tire popping.

I had hit a pothole.

I cursed. Really cursed.

Sage came riding back.

We stood for a long time staring at my tire. It was a full blow-out.

CHAPTER

We stood there, staring at my useless bike. Neither one of us knew what to do. We didn't have spare tires sitting around.

I squeezed the flat tire. The black rubber yielded limply.

Sage spoke first. "Can you fix it?"

I shook my head, feeling hollow and stunned.

"Maybe we could take your dad's bike," Sage suggested.

"I can't," I said. "It's too tall."

I needed another bike. Then it hit me.

"I have a plan." I said. "Wait here." I pushed my bike back to the building and carried it down the stairs. I dropped it next to the rack.

Then I took a deep breath and looked down at my fate.

The Uni-cycle.

There it was: glittery, streamers, the large shimmering head of a unicorn, grinning triumphantly. And of course the Uni-cycle was unlocked, because who would dare to steal such a noble beast?

I took another deep breath before reaching out a hand to touch it. What else was there to do?

My hand closed around the glittery frame. I pulled it up the stairs, doing my best to avoid getting coated in glitter. I tried not to imagine myself riding this creature, not to think about all the people who would be staring at me.

When I pushed it out the back door, Sage squealed with laughter.

"Yes!" she said. "Unicorns are magic. We'll be fine now."

"Only if we hurry," I said. "This is a one-speed."

Sage looked down at her watch. "10:44."

Sage and I rode down the alley to the street, headed towards the Greenway. I pedaled as fast as I could, leading the way, but the Uni-cycle was slow. Really slow.

People called and shouted comments at me just like they did at Michael. I could feel my cheeks burning, but not as much as my thighs already were. The bike was not made for speeding recklessly to a proposal.

The sun was hot, but we created our own breeze. The wind filled my ears. We had to make it. We had to.

Sage continued to yell updates, each one reminding me how much further behind we were falling. Why couldn't this thing go any faster?

Sage called 11:02 just as we began the descent down the ramp, to merge onto the Greenway. I barely noticed the continued pointing and catcalling. I focused on the Girard Street exit where Dad and Michael would be standing.

We rode under bridges, past other bikes rolling along.

Not long now. Finally, I could see it up ahead, the Girard Street ramp that led to Uptown.

"What time is it?" I called to Sage.

"11:08," she yelled back. "We're late."

I scanned for Dad and Michael. They should have been standing right there up ahead at the foot of the ramp. My stomach sank.

They weren't there.

I slowed my pace, calling back to Sage, "We missed them."

I rolled to a stop. The sun beat down on us. Without the wind of riding, I could feel my shirt begin to stick to the sweat on my back.

Sage pulled up next to me, staring ahead. "Wait," she called. "There they are." She pointed up the ramp. I followed the line of her finger.

Dad and Michael were at the top of the ramp, walking back into the noise and pavilions of the festival. They disappeared into the crowd.

I stood up on my pedals. "Let's go."

We pedaled as fast as we could up the steep ramp. Sage and I dismounted, pushing our bikes through the crowd. Not as many people were staring at us up here. There was so much else going on.

The festival was packed. People pressed around us. The air smelled like fried food and wood smoke. Booths filled with paintings, photos, jewelry lined both sides of the street. The sun glittered across tables of colored glass.

We pushed our way forward, but Dad and Michael could be anywhere.

We had to find them, but where?

"Could you just call and ask your Dad where he is?" Sage shouted over the noise of the crowd.

Call him. Why didn't I think of that? What the

heck was I doing, pedaling here at high speed, frantic? I had a cell phone. In all the hubbub, I had completely forgotten about it.

I reached into my pocket and pulled out my phone. I pressed it to my ear as the phone rang once, twice, three times. It forwarded to voicemail. Dad probably couldn't hear his phone in the noise of the festival.

I scanned over booths and food vendors. Then I saw the giant lemon-shaped lemonade stand. Yes. Michael could be there, ordering his radiant lemonade. I pushed towards it, scanning the people in line.

Nothing.

Think. Think.

Michael had probably bought the lemonade as soon as he had arrived. He might even have bought a refill by now.

"We need to find the port-a-johns," I called to Sage, following a crazy idea.

"What?" Sage asked.

"Follow me," I said.

It wasn't long before we found the line of port-a-johns, ten of them standing side by side. I pushed the Uni-cycle towards the line of people waiting to enter.

I saw them. Michael leaning against Dad, holding the empty cup in his hand.

I leaned the Uni-cycle against my leg and threw my hands over my head. I meant it as a way to wave to Dad. But Sage stood next to me, doing the same.

"Just like the painting," she said. "Victorious."

Dad turned and saw me. His face burst into a smile.

I pushed the Uni-cycle through the crowd.

"I'm here," I called to them. "We made it."

It was then that Michael turned his head. He looked from Sage, to me, to the Uni-cycle. He shrieked. "Jeremiah!" He said it like there was going to be more to what he said. But there wasn't. He just stood there, his mouth open.

Dad turned around, his eyes lighting up. "I

thought you backed out."

I shook my head.

"I tried stalling, but Michael here..." Dad jerked his head towards the port-a-johns.

Michael looked from me to Dad like he was trying to figure out what we were talking about.

"I have something for you." I unzipped my pocket and pulled out the box, handing it to Dad.

Michael stared at the box, his mouth still open. "Is this..." he asked, his voice trailing off.

Dad opened the ring box, the line of diamonds glittering in the hot sun. He got down on one knee, right there in front of the port-a-johns.

"Michael," Dad said. "This isn't exactly how I planned, but will you marry me?"

Michael had his hands on his cheeks. "Oh my god," he said. He looked at Dad. Then he looked over at me. "Omigod. Really?"

"Really," Dad said, rising to his feet.

"Of course I'll marry you!" Michael yelled at Dad. Dad slid the ring onto Michael's finger.

Michael wiped his eyes and pulled Dad into a kiss.

Several people around us clapped and cheered. For a moment I had forgotten about the crowd. A bunch of people were watching.

Sage and I looked at each other. I could feel myself blush.

"Wow," Michael said. He held up his hand sparkling in the light of the sun. He looked at Sage and me.

Dad leaned toward Michael for another kiss, but Michael pushed him away.

"Stop," Michael said. "I need to pee."

He darted into a port-a-john. Dad laughed and pulled me into a hug.

When Michael emerged, he gave Dad that second kiss.

"And you two," Michael said, turning to Sage and me. "I don't know what to say. I'm buying you guys some lemonade."

"Hallelujah," Sage said.

"Yeah," I said. "That sounds good."

"Radiant," Dad said.

I smiled. "Radiant."

ACKNOWLEDGMENTS

Writing a book is like growing a garden. There were many tasks and I needed a lot of help. Thank you to all that helped this book to grow.

First of all, I'd like to thank Dr. Sarah Park Dahlen for opening my mind to writing for justice and for introducing me to the scholarship of Michael Cart and Christine A. Jenkins in *The Heart Has Its Reasons* which started the seed of a story within me.

Thank you to my old neighborhood of Stevens Square, and to Metro Transit for providing such a fertile environment to work in. I wrote my first drafts of this book while riding the bus to and from class on public transit between Stevens Square, Minneapolis and Saint Paul.

I offer my sincerest thanks to my partner, Kris, and my dear friend, Abbie, who helped me to clear away the rocks and plastic until the story could breathe. And Rachel Joy, who helped the budding words to bloom.

Thank you, Stephen Fraser, for believing and finding the right place to plant my manuscript. Many thanks to Fian Arroyo for the abundant illustrations. And to Keith Garton and the team at One Elm for welcoming and watering my story until it could mature.